THE DRESS CIRCLE MURDERS

by

Peter Yates

A FIVE STAR MYSTERY

Full Length
Never Before Published

WILDSIDE PRESS

This book is produced in full compliance with government wartime regulations regarding the conservation of paper and other materials.

THE DRESS CIRCLE MURDERS

CHAPTER ONE

As long as I live, I shall feel strangely haunted whenever the 27th of a month falls on a Wednesday. I will remember always the year that Wednesday the 27th fell in October. It was a warm, heavy day for so late in the fall; the heat of the sun filtered into the city through a thick mist of restless, lowering clouds. As the day ended the invisible sun sank with blistering reluctance, making way for a cold silver moon, which rode triumphantly up the sky like a cutting blade, obscured now and again by hurrying shreds of fog.

It was natural enough that I should be thinking of Michael Rawn that day. It was the day that would end with the opening night of his play; the play Mike had written and in which he was to play the stellar role, the part he had written especially for himself. I am a newspaperman and no mystic; yet about Michael Rawn I had recognized from the first that indefinable something, that mystery of unplumbed depths, that is one of the surest signals of greatness. I felt this quality in Michael and was proud. For five years, Michael Rawn had been my best friend.

Three of us had come to New York together from college—Mike Rawn, Johnnie Olds, and myself, Sanford Blunt. We were green, but we knew then what we wanted. Michael Rawn was going to write and act in his own plays. John Olds was going to become a famous painter. I merely wanted to become a good newspaperman.

Three years before that memorable Wednesday we had carried our suitcases from Penn Station over to Broadway and had started north. Mike stopped us before a big glass window.

"Look," he commanded, "an Automat. You put in nickels and food comes out. That's us. I'm hungry."

We went in and put our bags on chairs and returned to the table shortly, laden with food. As we ate Mike began again.

"Now, if we want to make out all right," he determined, "we have to plan. We're not going to starve in the Village like you read about. We're going to get jobs to support our real work, until our interests can support us." Johnnie and I nodded. It sounded like good sense.

That afternoon we found a small apartment in the West Seventies. Johnnie Olds and I still lived there. Johnnie worked for his

3

living at the newspaper office, but he wasn't really interested. What he loved was messing around at night at the studio where he studied painting. John Olds had lots of talent and was coming along; you could see his work growing in skill and authority. I made out all right too at the *New York Globe;* I loved it from the start. My work was my whole life. At the end of three years I was at a desk receiving the foreign news on a radio receiving set and transcribing it to paper for the rewrite man, and hoping for a chance at feature writing.

Mike was something else again. In three years he had moved twice; changed jobs as many times, and now his play had struck. Mike hadn't changed. We saw him often. When he had moved the first time he wanted us to move in with him; he would take up the slack in the bigger rent. John didn't like the idea, so I let it ride. Now they were showing four-color spreads of Mike's new Park Avenue apartment in the slick magazines. It had been that easy for Michael Rawn. We had all applied at the *Globe* for jobs, but the starting wage had discouraged Mike, and he finally went to work at night in the Reservation Bureau at New York Central, doing his writing in the daytime. Mike didn't like the work, but he was a copywriter in a year. From there he went up like a sky-rocket.

Nothing was ever very hard for Mike, so I was not too surprised about the play. He could work like a devil beset, and thought of nothing but what he had to get done. Somehow events seemed to range themselves in his way like a row of dominos; all Mike had to do was to touch the first one.

Tonight the last domino would fall, and tomorrow, if Mike's luck held, he would be all he had meant to become when we bought our one-way tickets to New York.

It was Wednesday, October 27th. At five o'clock I sat at my receiving desk with my set off, dreaming of how little time it had taken Mike to come to the foot of his rainbow, when the voice of my chief, Pat Curry, cut through the pink clouds.

"Was it you, Blunt, who said you knew this young Michael Rawn?"

I looked up into his reflecting glasses, perched on his red face like tiny mirrors on an apple. You never saw his eyes for the light on those glasses, but nothing ever went past Pat Curry's shrewd eyes.

"Sure I know Mike Rawn. His roommate in school. We came to New York together; shared a flat."

The shiny red apple of Pat Curry's face tilted quizzically in my direction. "Think you could get an exclusive?"

The other receivers looked up. I smiled, but my heart bumped a little quicker.

"Yes," I answered slowly, "I think so."

Curry's retort was brisk. "See what you can do tonight; we might use it." He didn't wait; just walked away, and I went feverishly back to my work. It was my chance. No one in New York knew Michael Rawn as well as I did, I knew that. I couldn't miss. I thought of how my name would look above my own stuff, a by-line . . . by Sandy Blunt. Good. I would corner Mike when Johnnie and I went backstage. Pat Curry's voice jerked me into the office again.

"Better get home and into that rented tuxedo if you're going to cover an opening tonight . . ." He grinned at me, a white split in the apple, then turned savagely on the rest of the office. "All right! Let's get out the news . . .," then turned to me sternly, "And get back here with some exclusive dope on that wild-man you say is your friend." I was hoisting into my topcoat in the hall before the echo of his voice died.

Johnnie and I didn't have to rent tuxedoes, but we were wearing the same ones we had bought for the fraternity dances at school. We talked about Mike that night as we dressed.

. "I don't know about you, Sandy," John's quiet face smiled wryly, "but to me it's been just a minute since we got here. I suppose to Mike it's been a thousand years. Everything has to go fast to suit Mike."

"He just knew from the start what he wanted; size, shape, color, and how many." I struggled with my tie. "Mike said we had to start at the bottom; we did. Fact is that Mike was red-hot for this kind of thing—city achievement—from the day he was born."

"Sometimes I think Mike must have done some handsome acting when he was living with us," Johnnie considered. Johnnie never quite liked Mike as well as I did, but he was an artist, and I allowed for some professional jealousy.

"Maybe," I admitted, more to keep the peace than to agree, "but whatever he did, you have to admit he hasn't changed any."

There was a pause, and John said slowly, "Maybe Michael Rawn felt he didn't need to change any for just the two of us."

I didn't answer. After all, when you are more or less in the same field of endeavor, it must rankle when a friend forges ahead so fast. I had to go on living with John Olds, so I kept quiet. But I

5

was to recall what Johnnie had said, much later, and to give it deep thought.

"Well," John gave his tie a final yank before the bathroom mirror, "I have to hand it to Mike, at that. He said he would, when we were in school. He has it coming, I suppose. But I certainly thought it would take a whale of a lot longer."

"You have to give Mike ten for working," I commented. "He earns whatever he gets."

Mike Rawn had always been popular. He was thin and small and his face was bony and pale. But when those great brown eyes under his dark reddish hair came into a room, people looked up. Michael Rawn carried a flame in his face. I used to study the reaction to Mike, trying to make it tell me a story. It was hard, because I was Mike's closest friend. The nearest I ever got to an explanation was the single word *remote*. Mike seemed always, for all his friendliness and attention to others, to live in some curious withdrawal. When he listened, it made his interest seem the more flattering, for you had lured him from some quiet fastness of his own. This natural quietness made Mike easy to live with; he knew when to talk, when to keep quiet.

As I adjusted my suspenders I contemplated Mike Rawn and what his life would become after tonight. It was actually just the start; perhaps, I mused, for both of us. Strange, that my best friend was to be my first personal interview. Mike had laughed once when we had talked about it.

"Hell, Sandy," he bantered, "when I'm being interviewed, you'll be winning the Pulitzer Prize!"

But here it was, and I was interviewing Mike, who had arrived. Not for a minute did I dream of Mike as anything but a success. With his ability and that capacity for work and his natural charm, Mike was set. The rest would be downhill. The interview would be the start of the climb for me. So in different ways, Mike and I were beginning together. I yanked my shoes on, grinning. In a way, it was a double dream coming true.

I was brushing my coat when the buzzer rang, and I heard Johnnie swear as he ran to answer it. At the sound of the deep familiar voice I tore, coat and brush in hand, into the studio room.

"Mike! For God's sake, Mike; you ought to be at the theater! It's late, isn't it?"

Mike was smiling, his face boyish and happy. "It's only a little after six, and I'm not a bit nervous. Give me a cigarette. Well, are

6

you both glad?"

John Olds laughed and replied, "If you don't mind, Mr. Rawn, I'll go on shining my shoes. I'm going to a very important opening tonight."

We all laughed. Johnnie was pleased, and so was I, that Mike had come to see us on this night of all nights. Mike joined me in a cigarette. As he puffed I watched him, amazed again that this skinny friend of mine was on the eve of becoming famous.

Mike's eyes sparkled with excitement, but there was no nervous gesture; no wagging foot, no unnecessary movement. He sat controlled and at ease, smoking as he always did, deeply and leisurely, nodding as John told about a day at the *Globe*. With his faceted face and that dark red hair, it occurred to me now that Mike was an arresting looking kid, for all his short thinness. He would always look young. I found it difficult to see Mike as a stranger. In that one moment, however, I felt that here was a personage, had always been, and I was honored to be his friend. Mike might be vain, self-centered in his work; but that is common with people who strive toward a goal.

"How are you going to get to the theater in time?" Mike was so much of us that I had a sudden picture of him taking the subway to the theater where his name was in lights.

"Oh, Mr. Cushman, the producer, loaned me his car and chauffeur," Mike responded. It was a natural explanation, and Mike said it without any air.

"I have to hand it to you, Mike," Johnnie admitted, "you took this town by the tail and tied it in a knot. And the town liked it."

"That's nice enough, Johnnie," Mike pointed out practically, "but that's still to be proven. Tonight will tell. I really came here to invite you to a party at my new apartment after the show."

Johnnie said, just a shade too quietly, "The Park Avenue place in the magazines?"

I broke in; I could feel John trying to find a hint of condescension. "We'll be there with bells on," I accepted, "and before I forget it; I want to ask a favor, Mike. My boss wants me to get an exclusive on you; may mean quite a lot to me. How about it?"

Mike met my eyes and smiled. "Of course, Sandy! That's the reason I'm doing all this! So we can go up together, all of us! But you won't fail me now; about the party?" Mike looked almost imploringly at Johnnie, and with a trace of exasperation John put one hand on Mike's shoulder, slightly below his own.

7

"Sure I'll be there; we both will. You know we couldn't miss it."

Somehow I especially wanted this night to be flawless for Mike Rawn.

"I'm waiting to get a close look at those Broadway babes," I sang out, "but don't get me wrong! I don't understand why, with the swells you know, Mike, you still hang around with the peasants!"

Mike's thin face went serious, his eyes darkening.

"Don't make any mistake about me, you two. This won't go to my head. I planned my life this way; it's no surprise, no Cinderella story." He paused; then spoke again, slowly, as though out of some memory he had hidden for a long time. "I wasn't always this happy; with friends . . . or anything . . ." He suddenly took a deep breath, as though a load had been taken from his shoulders; he smiled at us both. "You were with me when we started; we began together. No ups or downs can come before that. That's the big thing; we came here together. I told you that a long time ago."

Johnnie stomped into his shoes. "Only three years ago," he reminded.

"Listen, Johnnie," Mike said succinctly, "I said in school I'd do this; now why is the fact of it so amazing? New York is a city full of people, just like any other place. Aren't we the same as we always were?"

"John feels nasty; his painting doesn't please him—too slow," I joked, trying to catch Johnnie's eyes. Mike turned to me.

"No, Johnnie isn't feeling nasty; he couldn't before the little I've done," Mike remarked trenchantly. "John is the one of us with the real talent, because he's a perfectionist, which I'll never be. It isn't so hard to do what I've done, when what you want is money."

Johnnie Olds looked mollified, so I kept quiet. I didn't point out that in New York or anywhere else, you usually gave out plenty of talent and work before you got that money, but this wasn't a time for long discussions.

"Oh, yes," Mike reminded himself, "this is the new address. It's a debut for the house, too. I just moved in this morning, bag and baggage. 340 Park Avenue, Apartment 13-C. The old offer of living together doesn't go any longer!" Mike winked at us with mock suggestiveness. "I'll tell you about everything at the party. Sandy, you want something exclusive; boy, you'll get it!"

"What's the surprise?" I demanded.

"I won't say a word; it's exclusive with the *Globe* . . . give you

8

the whole dope tonight," Mike smiled secretively at me. "Tell you tonight—on Park Avenue—the top of the world. . . ."

I smiled and nodded, and brought out a bottle of Old Forrester from the bureau drawer.

"Johnnie and I bought it to celebrate, and tonight is the night, Mike." I mixed us three very light ones. "Frankly, Mike, I used to wonder if you'd get all those things you had set your heart on. Now I know better than to wonder at all!"

We took our glasses and stood up. John crossed again to Mike and threw an arm about Mike's shoulders.

"Mike," John Olds looked directly into the dark eyes, "I've been holding out on you and I'm sorry. Clear the boards. I was sore; I suppose a bit jealous . . ." He lifted his glass quietly and with simple sincerity. ". . . to Michael Rawn, the next famous New Yorker; may all his work be as good as his best . . ." John drank and Mike and I smiled over our glasses.

As we put down our glasses, I glanced again at Mike. His eyes were wet. Somehow, my heart went out to him. Orphaned, always working and striving, able and creative, he would rise to truly great heights. Yet there was something sad about Mike's ability. I always felt an urge to protect him from something; I could hardly tell what.

Mike took a deep breath, as though he were about to plunge into a cold bath, and turning to us, smiled. He turned up his wrist to look at the time, and I saw now that he was wonderfully dressed, that his watch was new.

"Treat yourself to a new watch?"

"Yes," Mike admitted, smiling sheepishly. "A good one. Just in case the ship doesn't come in tonight, I'll have something to pawn."

We all laughed again. We were happy, and it felt good to be together on this particular night. But I saw the watch was a Patex-Phillippe. Anyone who buys one knows watches, and will go barefoot before he pawns it. Mike wasn't the barefoot type. He was planning on success.

We went to the door with Mike, lingering there, as though we were saying good-bye to something that was leaving us all.

"Good-bye, and God bless you, and good luck, Mike," Johnnie said, huskily, taking Mike's arm in a quick grasp.

Mike looked up at John dumbly, then muttered, "Thanks, Johnnie."

"Loads of the best, Kid," I gave Mike's other arm a hard pressure. Mike would always, in his vast enthusiasm, seem like a younger brother to me. He caught my eyes now, his look meaningful.

"I'll be all right; you'll see. I won't fail . . . " He said it almost grimly, his eyes gleaming in the dim hallway. "This is my lucky day. Remember how I used to say three was lucky for me? Three and nine? Well, look at the date! Three nines and the third day of the week! I can't miss!"

It was the light touch we needed just then, and we laughed together as Mike quickly ran down the three flights of stairs. John and I leaned over the railing watching him go, listened to the front door opening, heard a big motor start up. We went slowly back into the flat.

"I'm going to have a stiff one right now," John Olds reflected. "I need it. Why? Don't ask me! I'll just never really believe he's a mere human being. Three years. Holy God!"

I took my drink and stood before our calendar, thinking; not seeing a thing. Then I took a deep swallow of the drink John had handed me, and studied the dates on the paper before my eyes. Mike was right. The third day, Wednesday. And three nines, the twenty-seventh. Wednesday, the 27th. That October was neither the ninth month nor the third would not disturb Michael Rawn. It just wouldn't occur to him. I wondered if somehow this wasn't a careless key to Mike's story, to his success as far as he'd gone. I wondered again about all the various people in the part of Mike's life that John and I had not shared, the life that would rise to its first crescendo tonight.

I walked to the window and looked out of the well of the court, up at the sky. The moon, hidden now by clinging veils of dark cloud, swam its implacable, cold way across the heavens. A sudden thought jarred me. I had heard all of Mike's future plans; from the day I first knew Mike he had dreamed of success in New York. Tomorrow, always tomorrow, and what it would bring. But of Mike's youth, his yesterdays, I knew nothing. He never spoke of it. He was an orphan; that was all I knew.

I reminded myself to try to question Mike tonight, to learn something completely new about him if I could. And I must not forget that secret he had promised to tell me. I glanced back at the calendar. I hoped Wednesday the 27th would treat Mike right. I hoped he would find his luck. I decided to memorize the date.

I needn't have tried so hard. I was never to forget it. For Wednesday, October 27th, flung me into a maelstrom of horror and tragedy that changed my life in many ways, and through which I barely came out alive.

CHAPTER TWO

For an added thrill, Johnnie and I got out of the taxi at Broadway and walked west the half-block to the theater, joining the crowd that started toward the show-house crowned by the name MICHAEL RAWN, spelled out in those wonderful glowing bulbs that quicken or break so many hearts.

Just ahead of us a woman turned to her escort and said with rich finality, "But my God, Waldo, he's only twenty-three or four! I call that damn young!"

Johnnie nudged me and winked, muttering under his breath, "Me too, lady . . ."

But once in our seats a strange fear overcame both of us. We sat together, huddled into our shoulders, our palms wet. After I could stand it no longer, I leaned toward John.

"Scared?"

He nodded emphatically. "Suppose they don't like Mike? After all, they're not us."

I couldn't answer—just agreed with a miserable jerk of my head. By the time the lights went down we were both pretty sick.

The first act dialogue spun along through the late arrivals, setting the background for a younger brother, a member of the family we watched on the stage. The voices of the cast gradually quieted the audience. I found myself paying strict attention; already the play had begun to move, to breathe. I began to wait for this young man they talked about, upon whom so much in their stage lives depended.

Then, almost unnoticed, Michael came onto the set. I drew my breath in and held it, waiting for a blow to fall. Nothing happened. No catastrophe occurred because my friend, Mike Rawn, was walking and talking before a throng of strangers. As Mike began to speak my breath slipped out, and I started to listen again. It seemed natural, strangely actual, a reality now that Mike had come.

With the impact of a physical blow a fact caught me. Mike was at home! From that mouth came Mike's deep voice, clear and carrying, subtly inflected, meaningful—but somehow so completely *practiced,* so veteran. I felt at once a total stranger to this Michael Rawn. His voice pushed at the others on the stage, moving them toward an end he alone knew. It was fantastic and terrible. I felt Mike using the whole houseful of his stage family, using us in the audience, with that

11

deadly ease a snake employs with a bird. Mike's acting was pure nature. It was genius, and art could never improve it. And I was suddenly certain that Mike knew. He knew; it was no gamble for him. I thought of his clothes—of the new watch. I riveted my eyes on Mike; growing, dominating, building so surely, secure as the first act curtain fell.

There was a breathless pause, a sudden crack in the silence, then the thunder poured through, rolling and rolling. Johnnie beside me was smiling, and I was grinning foolishly back at him, and we were banging our hands like lunatics.

In the second act the action went forward briskly; the character Mike played came into the open with his schemes, and defied his family. It was ugly, and fascinating. This time the applause was not surprised, and it lasted longer. It had become a tribute. Johnnie motioned to me and we went out for a smoke.

"Well!" His face lit with happy relief.

"It's all right now," I wagged my head in agreement, "he's really got it, now!"

As we went back to our seats John and I looked around to see if we knew anyone. The house was packed, but over on the left was a box with just one person in it.

"Wonder who that is?" I indicated the large figure above us.

"Some socialite, I guess; only one who could afford an opening night box to himself."

All around us, over the audience, people were leaning across one another, talking, pointing. I sat down and watched the motionless figure in the dress-circle box. His eyes seemed fixed on a spot beyond the curtain, on the stage behind it. With a newsman's eye I noted that he was nearly bald, that for all his huge bulk there was about him a feeling of strength, of firmness about that aquiline nose and the steady mouth. He was, even seated, a man of imposing size in both bone and flesh. I was still looking at him as the lights went down for us to see the ending of Mike Rawn's first attack on the Big City.

It was, to put it simply, a knockout triumph for Michael Rawn. His stage family cornered him in the end, and by every human impulse you should have felt glad. But somehow Mike made you sorry for him, and as the play ended you felt like defending him from the monsters of respectability and decency. It gave the play itself a peculiar twist, but it was a tremendous display of Mike's talent. The curtain sped down amid applause that rose like a tidal wave. People began to stand, here and there, and at last the whole house stood, beating its hands in perfervid demonstration. For minutes we kept at it; then like a quiet boy, Michael Rawn came before the curtain, alone.

He smiled, that simple smile I knew so well, easy and genuine. They liked him, and Mike accepted it without fanfare or spurious amazement, as he would have accepted failure.

"There is only one thing I could say to you tonight that would mean anything," Michael Rawn said to them, his dark eyes roving over the audience as though we were all one person, "and that is just . . . . thank you very much."

They went wild. Mike bowed once very low, and then turned and bowed directly at the man who sat alone. "Bravo!" the big man cried, rising, and Mike bowed to him again, and disappeared between the curtains. The applause died, the buzz of talk resumed. Johnnie and I fought slowly up the aisle toward our coats.

I decided that it would be useless to try to see Mike backstage. Johnnie hailed a taxi and we set off for Mike's Park Avenue address. As we settled back I expelled a deep breath and surreptitiously caught a look at John's profile. He seemed to be studying types along the street.

"Well, now that it's safely over; what did you really think of it?"

"I'll tell you, Sandy." He paused, then went on slowly. "I think we've seen a virtuoso performance the like of which only Mike could produce. It was art; it must have been. True, actual, conscious art; genius if you like. Yet there is something dream-like about Mike; about the play itself. I can hardly explain it; it's just a feeling. It's something very personal in Mike himself, something he did without meaning to do it at all. I don't quite understand myself, my feelings about it. But I'd go back to see it; I like whatever it is . . . ."

Gazing out of the window I agreed, haltingly. "Yes. He's good. But I understand. I couldn't describe it, either—a strange quality—something great inside that I never knew he had."

"He's certainly cinched his first step up the ladder," John reflected. "It seems a shame such slow dimwits as I am have to live. Mike does things so damn easily. . ." He turned and flashed me a brief smile. "Don't mind me; just pure jealousy!"

I punched him lightly on the arm. "Don't let it get you, John, my friend," I advised. "You've got just as much. Take it from me, word-punching is easier than this business with brushes. Work is what it needs. And time."

Johnnie returned to gaze at the expensive desertion of Park Avenue. "Yeah," his voiced edged with bitterness. "Sure. But how much?"

The cab halted smoothly before a marquee, and the doorman opened the door. I paid and we walked into the lush lobby. We gave our floor; the operator repeated it as a compliment. We swooped up.

"Penthouse, gentlemen," the operator said as he opened the door with a flourish. Johnnie turned to me with a sour look, and shrugged.

"*First* stop; a Park Avenue penthouse," he announced to no one in particular.

I said nothing. I was a bit amazed myself. Thirteen-C was to the left, and almost before we knocked a butler had opened. A polite surge of conversion ebbed to meet us. We deposited our coats in a dressing room and went down two steps into the living room.

Mike did not seem to be there yet, but no one paid anyone much attention. John and I ranged through the gabbling mob that had already assembled to drink the liquor and eat the bread of success. I began to wish that I had stuck to my original plan of seeing Mike at the theater, because it would be just as hard to get to him in this crush. Johnnie had spotted a likely looking blonde in a red dress, and with a wink was off a-hunting. I picked a drink from a tray and made for the buffet for a piece of cold turkey. I leaned against the buffet and turned for a careful look about the room.

The living room was two-storied and large. Everything was new and obviously expensive. On the far wall a curving stair led to a balcony onto which opened what I guessed to be the bedroom doors. To my left was the fireplace wall, on which were two doors thrown wide onto a terrace; for the night, while misty, was not too cool. To my right two steps led up onto the foyer and the door through which we had just came. It was an apartment built for entertaining.

Rather in spite of myself, my eyes returned to the broad fireplace wall to my left. It was a stark, modern wall, cut by the fireplace opening and the two flanking terrace doors, and dominated by an enormous oil portrait of Michael. It was fully life-size, and full-length, and its background made it at the very least ten feet tall. It was magnificent and it was Michael, but I did not like it. I guessed it must be fashionable and well done, or Mike would not have had it in his new apartment. As I stood idly looking over the heads of the crowd, a lovely voice right beside me startled me into turning.

14

"If you'd move just an inch or two," the voice greeted, "I could reach that plate of pickles."

I stood for a moment speechless. I stayed right where I was an instant, then smiled.

"Here, let me help you." I got a plate and helped her to food, making a lingering torture of it. She was a blonde with hair, heavy and dark gold, and a skin the color of vanilla caramel. You knew she tanned beautifully. Her mouth was wide and humorous, and a quick glance told me she had the figure I like; a tapering waist, long thighs, and round hips. I looked down into deep blue eyes.

"What's your name, little girl? Are you a friend of the family?"

She looked up at me evenly, I started to drown in those eyes. I've often had my feet wet, but never felt myself happily going under like this. Then she held up her left hand. On it was a large diamond.

"My name is Engagement Ring; Miss Ring to you," she said levelly. All at once I knew this was no girl with whom I would banter nothings. I wanted to talk to her.

"I'm sorry; I didn't mean to be crude," I offered. "My name is Sandy Blunt of the *Globe*. I'm a good friend of Michael Rawn's."

Her mouth moved slightly with some emotion I could not quite fathom, then her brows lifted.

"You mean to tell me Mike didn't tell you?" she queried. "My name is Lisa Cushman. Papa produced Michael's play." She held out a slim hand and I took it. Her handclasp was firm; I liked it. She smiled and moved away at once.

I followed her with my eyes. For no reason at all I was dissatisfied with the party; I hated it. It seemed full of meaningless noises, bird-calls of empty gaiety. And for the first time I could understand John's feeling of helplessness before the ordered march that was the life of our great friend, Michael Rawn. The ring; the perfect, expensive diamond ring. The Boss' daughter. Lisa Cushman was Mike's secret, of course. Mike was going to announce their engagement tonight. That was to be my exclusive. I almost left the party, but I caught sight of that heavy gold hair, and it was coming through the crowd, toward me. She reached my side with an older, very handsome man in tow.

"I want you to know my father, Mr. Blunt," she stated.

"Sandy," I corrected. "Remember, I'm that old family friend."

She laughed, deep and strong. "Father, this is Sandy Blunt. He is Michael's very good friend."

"It's a very great pleasure, Mr. Blunt," he assured me, "I suppose

15

we'll be seeing a lot of you."

"I hope so," I smiled. "When do you expect Mike, Mr. Cushman? I have an interview with him tonight."

"I've been here since before the final curtain. I came over early just to get here before Mike," Lisa said, turning to her father. He seemed to be a bit mystified.

"I don't know where he is," he responded. "I went to his dressing room right after the performance, but he had left. I thought he was here, so I hurried along." A silent look passed between them.

"I guess he'll be along," I hazarded, and they shook my hand and moved off. I decided to wait around for Mike. He'd have to get here soon.

I caught sight of Johnnie and the blonde and followed them onto the terrace. The blonde seemed familiar but I couldn't place her.

"I suppose I'm superfluous?" I demanded. Johnnie didn't even reply, just nodded judicially.

I wandered away, admiring the lights below me, the glare from the room shielded by a tall potted pine shrub. As my eyes became accustomed to the dark, I became aware of a dark-haired woman standing near me. She was stunning, thin for my taste, but with poise and perfect carriage. She seemed young. I held out my cigarette case, and without a word she took one. She didn't thank me, just stood there holding it. The whole performance was becoming to her.

"Handsome view," I began.

Her voice was low and husky and vaguely familiar. "You didn't give me a light," she stated flatly, and I knew who she was—Martha Wain, Mike's leading lady. I lit the cigarette, leaning toward her.

"Sorry, Miss Wain," I apologized. "I didn't recognize you in the dark."

"Never mind," she said coolly. "With the Boy Wonder in full throttle, who would recognize anyone?"

"I'm an old friend of Michael Rawn," I said, quietly. She turned to look at me directly. I could see the whites of her eyes plainly.

"It's all right with me," she shrugged, "I never saw you before. What do you do? Theater?"

"I'm a newspaperman."

"Good," she approved, and turned away. I followed her.

"Don't you like Mike Rawn?" I ventured, standing close enough to get the perfume. She turned so quickly I nearly fell backwards.

"Listen, stooley," she directed, her voice dangerous as a loose razor blade, "Mr. Rawn is the most considerate star in the business; and go right and tell him I said so. And for yourself; go to hell!"

I stared after her, curious and surprised. Twice tonight, with the Cushmans, and now with Martha Wain, I had felt an undercurrent of feeling, an intimation of another life far different from the life I had thought was Mike Rawn's. Then I recalled that these were people of the theater, that jealousy rides them with the custom of ancient experience; an indissoluble entity, like a witch and her broom.

I finished my cigarette and decided to make some effort to locate Mike. I couldn't wait all night. I walked through the terrace door back into the living room, stuffy now with smoke. Just as I entered, my glance caught the foyer over the heads of the party, and I saw Mike. He was doing something very strange. He was leaving! Then I took a longer look. The lights were deceptively flattering, but I was certain it was Michael. I fixed my eyes on the figure in the foyer, coated, drawing on his gloves. It *was* Michael. But his hair was blond and short, cropped in a crew haircut. Two hours ago, on the stage, Mike Rawn had had dark reddish hair; Michael's hair! I started to push my way roughly through the busy mob of dancing, eating people. It was impossible! I wanted to talk to Mike now, very badly.

As I reached the front door I flung it open and called Mike's name. Across from me the elevator doors closed. For a long time I stood in the hall, scowling. It could have been the light; it must have been. Because it *was* Michael Rawn I had seen. Mike's hair often glinted in the sunlight. I felt a bit put out, for Pat Curry would want my story sometime before morning. Mike knew how important it was to me. I couldn't wait all night to file my story, even if it were a top feature.

I came back through the foyer, swearing under my breath, and looked up to find myself facing that image of Mike across the big room. All at once, inexplicably, I hated that portrait. It wasn't Mike at all. The artist had had a grudge against Mike, and Mike himself, perhaps out of his desire to own the portrait, had not cared how cruelly he had been defined. But there was something, a story, an arid coldness somewhere, that I did not like and could not segregate. I forced myself to look full into the face of the portrait. One thing at least was very clear. It had dark reddish hair.

My watch said one o'clock, and I looked for Johnnie, found him tucked away in the neat library, behaving artistically to his new blonde friend.

"Come on," I interrupted, "the hell with waiting for Mike. It's

17

back to the old desk for me. He didn't even show up. Give your friend your phone number, Johnnie, and put her on a siding. We're workingmen and it's late."

John nodded, kissed her for a long minute, and rose, her hand in his regretfully.

"It was very nice to have met you," he bowed politely, and we went to get our coats.

"Nice party after all," he continued, as we got into the elevator. We had the box to ourselves. I nodded shortly and he went on, puzzled, "See Mike at all? What's wrong? Didn't he come through?"

"I saw Mike leaving," I mumbled shortly.

"Leaving? Hell, when did he come? I wanted to give him my best; that was a helluva good play. . . ."

I was busy thinking as we walked through the lobby to our taxi. We rode home in silence. Johnnie wasn't too tight to know I didn't want to talk. At home, my tie loosened, I called Pat Curry.

"Curry? This is Blunt."

"Yea? Want a rewrite man. . .?"

"Wait. Listen. I don't know whether I got a story or not."

His voice rose like a geyser. "WHAT? I thought you said. . . ."

I was still trying to think in a straight line. I couldn't get rid of the feeling that I had inadvertantly seen something important.

"Maybe I got something bigger than what you sent me for."

"What the hell are you talking about, Blunt? Get straight and tell whatever. . . ."

"Listen," I directed slowly, "I'm not certain; I want you to check this carefully. . . ."

"Yea . . ." His voice was eager now, waiting. I reconsidered.

"I think I ought to come right down. I want to talk to you about something I saw."

"All right; take a cab," he ordered brusquely, as I hung up.

I sat under the hot green shade of his desk arc and told him everything I had seen, which seemed little enough. He studied me, his spectacle mirrors never leaving my face. When I had finished he rapped his knuckles on his desk.

"If you've uncovered something, it's damn good," he simmered, "but if this is a fake publicity stunt for Rawn, God help you."

I waited, sitting in my rumpled tuxedo as he dialed and talked again and again. I watched the electric wall clock jerk through fifteen

18

minutes, then thirty, as Pat Curry phoned the morgue, the hospitals; Martha Wain, the theater, Mr. Sam Cushman, Mike's apartment where a sleepy valet answered. Then he phoned the police and turned to me.

"Good work," he said almost dreamily. "I want you to go on from here." He sat smiling mirthlessly at me, the split of his teeth making his face a Hallowe'en apple.

I was trying to assimilate a fact I could hardly believe. Pat Curry's calls had proven evidence against my own senses. From the minute of his single curtain-call, no one had set eyes on Michael Rawn, dead or alive!

CHAPTER THREE

I went back to the apartment, but couldn't sleep. About 5 in the morning I took a cold shower and went down to the office. Pat Curry was still at his desk, facing the half-light of the coming day, staring out toward Tudor City and the East River. He looked up as I opened the door and whirled around in his swivel chair, fixing his opaque lenses on my face. Then he reached up and turned off the work light over his desk.

"Sit down here, Blunt."

I took the chair he indicated.

"I've been going over some of your stuff, Blunt. It's all right. I wonder if you really are a writer?"

I swallowed, then replied steadily, "I think so."

He nodded. "So do I. I think you'll make a damn good writer; and I think you've got your story. Just how well did you know this Michael Rawn?"

I had no need to ponder that question. "I was his roommate when he first came to Westminster College. Mike came in his Junior year. We were friends for two years there. I came to New York with him. It's been altogether almost six years."

There was a short pause, then he went on, his voice curt, almost giving directions. "All right. I'm taking you off that radio receiving desk. This is the stuff. I want to know everything about Michael Rawn; dead, alive, blackmail, murder, anything and all . . . . whatever has happened to him; that's your meat. You'll get an expense account, and keep out of the saloons. I want everything, if humanly possible or not. But I want it ALL. This has everything for big human interest—Cinderella suddenly disappears—get it? And whatever develops, you take it from there. And keep in touch."

"OK; I can do it," I told him.

"Get going," he jerked his head. "You're on your own."

"No reports since I was here last night?"

"None." Pat Curry pursed his lips and shook his head with gratification. "Your little college chum has completely disappeared. My guess is foul play, but you're the guy who is going to TELL ME—get it? Now, on your way."

I got up and took the elevator, deep in thought. As I got onto Forty-second Street the late morning editions were being loaded. Across a front page of one of the tabloids ran a big scarehead . . . . STAGE STAR VANISHES . . . above a picture of Mike, serious and large-eyed. I picked off a copy and walked to Third Avenue and at the Automat got coffee and some eggs. As I ate I turned to Mike's story.

Michael Rawn Missing; Foul Play Feared ran the inside head over the article. There was another picture of Mike, and beside it a picture of Lisa Cushman, reportedly engaged to the missing man. In overripe adjectives the story told briefly what I had witnessed the night before. Mike's quick success, his happy ending, love with the boss' daughter: the outline of a success story. I found nothing new; I had hardly expected anything at that.

I rose from the table and walked to the corner and took a cab home. As I paid the driver I came to a conclusion. I had known Mike Rawn well. Everything I knew of him was a picture of ceaseless struggle upward. Mike's was not the picture of a suicide, in any event.

As I entered the apartment, Johnnie sat up in bed.

"Well; what's the news?"

I began to undress slowly. "I want to get up when you go in the morning," I stated. "It'll give me a couple of hours, anyway."

"All right," John replied, "but what went on? Learn anything?"

"Nothing," I told him, "except that Mike has actually gone. Vanished into thin air; at the one time in the world when no one would want to go away. Pat Curry thinks something has happened to Mike; some kind of foul play. I'm still on it, whatever it is."

"Swell," John Olds said absently; then his voice went on after a pause, "I was thinking about Mike tonight, Sandy. When you get right down to his character, it's always been more or less mythological. The boy with the ambition who succeeds; and that's all . . ."

20

I agreed sleepily. "We don't know anything about Mike himself. But that's natural. When a person tells you his plans for the future you think you know him because he confides in you. You don't. You're just flattered; everyone likes being chosen as a confidant. Mike told us his plans; we thought we knew all there was to know about him. Now I have to find out what we didn't know."

We said good-night; John promised to waken me. It was six-fifteen and I had almost two hours to sleep. I was tired and it seemed a wonderfully long time.

I must have slept fitfully, muttering or snoring, because once I remember John's voice sharply shutting me up. I don't know when I had the dream, but it seemed I had been asleep for a long time.

It was a dream I used to have when I was very young, maybe four or five, and I hadn't had the dream since I grew up; not for years. It was one of my earliest memories. My father had taken me one day to the zoo, and like every kid, I climbed onto the rail to see the animals closer. As I stood there, one of the big cats turned and leaped toward me against the bars, snarling at a piece of meat in the trough before his cage. I screamed and cried, and for days dreamed of that cat as it had turned, its eyes direct and ravenous, crouching to leap at me. I would wake up cowering and dripping wet, screaming with the terror only a child can know.

That night I dreamed of the cat again. It turned suddenly, poised, gathered, knowing its terrible strength, staring into my horrified face with that unsubdued jungle cruelty. Silently it coiled and sprang, and this time it reached me. I struggled for my life against the beast, sweating with terror, trying to shriek for help with a throat horribly voiceless. I awoke with Johnnie, blessedly real, shaking my shoulder.

"Good Lord, Sandy; what's wrong with you?" He stood above me fully dressed. I leaned up and ran a hand through my hair.

"I must be going nuts," I observed. "Wow; what a dream!"

"Blonde?" John smirked.

"No," I answered curtly. I could never joke about that dream. It scared me too thoroughly.

In my nightclothes I went to the phone and hunted Mr. Sam Cushman in the book, and dialed his office.

"Cushman Productions," sang a cute female voice.

"Mr. Sandy Blunt, the New York Globe. I'd like an appointment. It concerns Mr. Michael Rawn."

"Oh, Mr. Rawn. . ." the voice diminuendoed into silence, then

21

swept flutteringly upward. "I'll get Mr. Cushman on the wire."

There was a long, empty pause; the voice returned. "Mr. Cushman is busy at the moment, Mr. Blunt. But he would be delighted to see you here in about one hour, say 10 o'clock. That suit, Mr. Blunt?"

"Thank you, that's fine."

"Ten o'clock, then, Mr. Blunt." The cuteness returned, fortissimo. I turned to John, who was eavesdropping.

"You don't have to go to the office today?" he questioned, and I nodded. "To fame and fortune," he added solemnly, "over Mike's dead body! Let me be the first to shake your hand."

I punched him in good humor. The whole thing was a break for me; I couldn't get around that part of it.

"You artistic guys are a flock of vultures."

With the apartment to myself I bathed and shaved slowly, savoring my time richly. My mind raced along, recalling small things, deliberately searching for the smallest item about my friend that might give me a clue to the inscrutable problem of his disappearance. I thought of Mike's popularity. He had been liked as well as any. What differences were there beyond his ambition that had made Mike unique? What small things?

Candy. Mike loved candy, expensive chocolates. Boston baked beans. Boxes of any shape and size, with well-fitting lids. They need not have anything in them at all; Mike just liked the neat fit. Black. Mike had liked black; black velvet under his hand, black sweaters, shoes, silk socks, black leather gloves, black-haired girls at school. With a sudden start I remembered Lisa Cushman's long blonde shank of hair. Mike had always been definite about black hair; black was his favorite color. Gadgets and devices he loved. Mike had kept in his drawers at school a vast array of can-openers, pencil-sharpeners, pen points, tie-clasps of any strange mechanical variety, numberless corkscrews—all unused. Mike never went home for holidays. He had no home, no parents, no relatives that I knew. What was his mother's maiden name? The thought itself puzzled me. Why had it come to me; his mother's name? Why should I wonder what it was? Then I recalled something Mike had told me ages ago. An aunt of his mother. His only remaining relative. He had never seen her. I had no idea where she might be found. That was it, all right; his mother's aunt was Michael Rawn's next of kin. And where could I begin to find her? I glanced at my watch; it was time to go.

Cushman Productions' suite in Rockefeller Center was a very handsome layout, all glass brick, low chairs, inlaid linoleum. The cute voice was dark-haired and sharp-eyed, her smile friendly.

She ran her eyes up and down me, and replied when I gave her my name: "Mr. Cushman is in conference, but I'll just give him a ring, Mr. Blunt. Please sit down."

Before I had warmed a chair she indicated a big door. As I entered the large office, Mr. Sam Cushman rose and held out his hand cordially.

"How do you do, Mr. Blunt? Glad to see you again so soon."

I got right down to business. "I've come to try to get a line on my friend, Michael Rawn. . ." I began. His face clouded, and I added, "but if there is something you'd like to tell me off the record. . ."

He waved his hand. "Not at all, Mr. Blunt." He paused, then went on carefully. "I hardly think I could be of much help. Naturally, for more than one reason, the disappearance of Michael Rawn at this time has upset me. The show is almost certain to close. Frankly, the part demands Michael; no one else will do."

"I can understand that, Mr. Cushman. Mike wrote it for himself. He didn't mean anyone else to play it."

Cushman smiled, wrinkling on either side of his blue eyes. "You must have known Michael very well. What you say is completely right. I feel that he will always write for himself, and good as that may be, it is limiting."

I came back to the point in hand. "Is there anything, the least detail, Mr. Cushman, that might make you feel that there had been foul play? Any disturbance in the cast, for instance?"

He seemed surprised, almost alarmed at my suggestion. "What do you mean, foul play?"

I deprecated my speech with a gesture. "Merely a suggestion, Mr. Cushman. What I meant was, has anything occurred during the time you have known and worked with Mike that might indicate to you a reason for his disappearance?"

Sam Cushman put his well-manicured fingers before him on the desk and studied them, announcing quietly, "No, Mr. Blunt, I know of nothing that might have made Michael Rawn an enemy. He was steady; a good trouper by nature. No effort was ever too much. He would take any sort of advice, and in good sort. Michael Rawn had a keen mind and was a hard worker; he had a very great future."

I smiled. "He *has* a great future. . . ."

Sam Cushman's blue eyes froze mine for a second.

"If you mean to imply that I did not like Michael Rawn, Mr. Blunt, you are very wrong." He smiled quietly. "Michael was to have become my son-in-law."

I rose and extended my hand. "Thank you very much, Mr. Cushman. I'm obliged to you for the time."

At the door he called to me: "Come back any time, Mr. Blunt. I'd like to do anything I can," he finished, rather lamely. I thanked him again and closed the door thoughtfully behind me.

The girl at the switchboard was staring at me curiously. I gave her a smile and stopped on my way into the hall.

"I'm interested in finding my friend, Michael Rawn. Perhaps you could help me, Miss. . ."

"Miss Kay McGonigle," she pealed.

"Miss McGonigle," I acknowledged. "Could you tell me anything that might help? Was Mike well liked? Just tell me something you remember; anything at all."

She puckered her brow, felt of her elaborate hairdress.

"Well, I just can't think of anything definite, Mr. Blunt; but I'd love to help. I can't think. . ."

I smiled again and urged her, leaning confidentially in her direction. "Well, now let's see, Miss McGonigle. Was there anyone who didn't like Mr. Rawn, for instance?"

"Oh, no! We all liked Mr. Rawn. He was very nice, not like some at all! I said so only this morning to Mr. Biglow, Mr. Rawn's valet, when he phoned. No; everyone liked Mr. Rawn."

"How long have you known about Mr. Rawn's engagement to Miss Cushman?" Love usually finds a way, I hoped.

Miss McGonigle dispatched a call and returned to me promptly.

"We all guessed, Mr. Blunt, for a long time. That Martha Wain hung around Mr. Rawn for quite a while, they used to go everywhere; but after Miss Cushman came along—well, Wain just didn't have a chance in a million." She pulled down two cords and added, "And speaking about people who don't like other people, well, just mention Martha Wain to anyone, Mr. Blunt, JUST MENTION HER!" She made a gesture like a seal refusing old fish. I put on my hat.

"Well, thank you very much, Miss McGonigle." I moved to the door. I had a sudden inspiration, and returned to the switchboard.

"Miss McGonigle, under ordinary circumstances, if Mr. Rawn fell ill, who would take his part?"

"Under ordinary circumstances, Mr. Blunt, it would be his un-derystudy's job. But that's just it! It ain't ordinary circumstances. Mr. Cushman wouldn't dream of letting Mr. Rawn's understudy play it. I know that! But that is the usual. . ."

I interrupted impatiently. "I know; but suppose Michael Rawn were out of the cast, the tickets were sold. . ."

Miss McGonigle broke in firmly. "No, Mr. Blunt. This play would not work that way. To tell the truth, this is an unusual case; Mr. Cushman said so himself. The play is built around the part Mr. Rawn plays. And Floyd Harvey couldn't do it in a month of Sundays."

"Floyd Harvey? Is that the understudy's name?"

"That's right," she nodded, "Floyd Harvey. But you see, Mr. Blunt, he was more of what they call a stand-in than an understudy. Sometimes Mr. Rawn would be working on the script and couldn't re-hearse; then Mr. Harvey just walked through the play so the rest of the cast could rehearse. But he couldn't act it in a million years!"

"Then why did they hire him?" It seemed illogical to me. "If he couldn't act he wasn't much good, was he, to anyone?"

"Oh," she shrugged, "in a production like this he came in plenty handy. Mainly it was his size that got him the job, Mr. Blunt. He was almost identical with Mr. Rawn, maybe a bit heavier. He could take Mr. Rawn's fittings and generally save time for Mr. Rawn in production. His size was the big thing; everyone on Broadway knows Floyd Harvey can't act worth beans!"

"Does Floyd Harvey know he can't act?"

Her contempt was like scalding gravy, dark and rich. "No bum actor knows it! And the bigger the ham, the more certain they get that their art is simply a mystery beyond the masses! Floyd Harvey got so hopped up on himself in Mr. Rawn's part he almost thought he *was* Mr. Rawn! He looked simply awful in that wig . . ."

I stared at her sharply.

"Wig?"

Miss McGonigle raised what was left of her brows. "Yes; *wig!* The last straw; if you ask me! Mr. Rawn has dark hair, and Floyd got a dark red wig to wear in case something happened—and everyone in town knew he would never play it if the world came to an end! Mr. Cushman would close the play first!"

"But Floyd Harvey bought a dark red wig?"

"Sure! That's the joke! Floyd Harvey has blond hair; he had

it all cut off—a crew cut just like a college boy—just so he could wear that dark wig! That's what's so funny, Mr. Blunt!"

CHAPTER FOUR

Pat Curry looked up as I entered.

"What's the matter, Blunt? Trouble?"

I stood for a moment looking out of a window, watching the garbage scows. "No trouble. I just don't know where to begin."

He spread his hands. "That's always the problem. It won't throw you. A good idea is to try the nearest of kin."

"That's no good on Michael Rawn," I faced him. "A great-aunt on his mother's side is the only living relative that Mike ever told me about. He never even saw her."

Curry was undisturbed. "No difference. It gives you a starting point. And you never know what you're going to learn. Get to this great-aunt and she may tell you something that leads you to someone else. Keep punching, that's all."

As I started toward the door he finished, ". . . and remember, it isn't the vanished person who makes the trouble for a reporter—it's the people he leaves behind him. Those are the birds you are looking for. Keep it in mind; you'll do all right."

"O.K." I answered.

He snapped his fingers in remembrance. "Oh, yes, Blunt. I almost forgot. There was a call for you. I'm taking your calls while you're on this thing. A guy named Valerian."

I came back to his desk and took the slip of paper he held out to me. "I don't know any Valerian. Did he leave a message; a number?"

"Nope. Said he'd get in touch with you. Smooth voice, full of the old culture."

"It's no one I know."

He shrugged. "Well, on your way, boy. Make it good."

I walked up Lexington Avenue and across to Park. I wondered who had called me. The name Valerian meant nothing to me, and if it were someone who wanted me badly they could have left a number.

The sighing elevator in Mike's building took me to 13-C. I buzzed, and after a long wait, the door opened very quietly, to reveal an old man with the kindest face I have ever seen. He was wrinkled and white-haired, but his complexion was pink and clear as a Havilland

26

saucer.

"I would like to speak to Mr. Biglow," I said, "I'm Sandy Blunt, Michael Rawn's oldest friend."

The old man opened the door wide in invitation. The living room looked much higher and wider now it was empty. The portrait of Mike dominated the polished flats and discreet decoration like a bomb in a glass factory.

"I am Biglow, Mr. Rawn's valet," the old man said at my elbow. "I'm glad you have come, Mr. Blunt. May I get you something to drink?"

I nodded, and he returned with a tall glass. It was hardly after noon, but I needed one. The light poured into the place and I was reminded of Grand Central's upper level. Without people this room was cold and bloodless, a perfection of taste and money; a lifeless elegance. It was not a home; simply a dumb display of decoration. I looked at Biglow, standing before me soundlessly, respectfully waiting.

I turned to him, glass in hand. "Biglow, do you believe that Mr. Rawn would commit suicide?"

To my surprise, the old man put his hands to his eyes; then slowly took them away. His face was streaked with sudden tears.

"No sir. I do not think so at all. I know of nothing at all that would cause Mr. Rawn to take such a step. Nothing."

"You liked Mr. Rawn very much?" I questioned gently.

It was a minute before Biglow answered. "I did, Mr. Blunt; I did indeed. I . . . worshipped Mr. Rawn. He was . . . kindness itself to me."

I pitied Biglow; it was so easy to understand how he would have loved Mike. With his elders Mike had always been kindness itself. I had a sudden memory of Mike at school, talking to the janitors, the housewives in town; people none of the rest of us ever knew existed.

"Biglow, I would like to go through Mr. Rawn's papers with you. Do you know where he kept them?"

Biglow nodded with pride in his voice. "Yes, Mr. Blunt. Mr. Rawn kept his important papers right here. He told me everything." He guided me up the stairs and along the balcony into a large corner bedroom. Biglow went to a wallhanging and lifted it. I saw a combination lock.

"Mr. Rawn kept his papers in here."

"Can you open it, Biglow?"

For answer, he applied to the dials, and I could hear him mumbling

27

to himself as he counted the pins dropping while he worked the combination. I waited beside a writing desk as Biglow crossed the room with the small armful of Mike's personal belongings.

Spread out on the writing desk, they seemed singularly uninteresting for so dynamic a character as Michael Rawn. As I went through them, they became more and more prosaic in the light of my attempt to find a clue to Mike's unexplained disappearance.

There was an annuity for a considerable sum, which interested me somewhat. I had had no notion that Mike had possessed so much money. There was a pack of old, dirty letters, tied in a shabby pink ribbon. An insurance policy, with Biglow the beneficiary. I picked up the pack of letters speculatively, then put them down. They were Mike's private life, and I had no right to look at them—not yet, anyway. For I did not actually know that Mike had been done away with; there might still be some explanation. I picked up the annuity and read it, and received a surprise. The next of kin was listed as Lady Matilda Wintarthur, 1099 Fifth Avenue, New York City. I motioned to Biglow that he could return the letters and the folders with the policies in the safe. I had got what I came for.

"Biglow," I asked, "did you know the name of Mr. Rawn's closest relative?"

He swung the hanging into place and turned.

"Yes, Mr. Blunt. Mr. Rawn told me himself. I called Her Ladyship this morning when I was convinced that—Mr. Rawn was not coming home."

"What did she say to your news?"

Biglow's face was emotionless. "She thanked me for the notification, and hung up."

"I see. Did you notify the police, Biglow?"

"Yes, I did, Mr. Blunt. At the same time I phoned to Her Ladyship. A bit later an Inspector Cassidy called me and told me to expect him sometime this morning or early afternoon. I thought when you rang it was he."

I smiled. "He's a good man, Biglow; he'll help you." I remembered Inspector Cassidy from the first days I had spent on the *Globe;* he had helped me a lot when I was still hanging around the precinct stations for handouts.

Smiling at my memories, I stepped into the adjoining bathroom. Unaccountably, once again I felt a sense of Mike's possession of money. The bath appointments were plain white; but the towels were thick and heavy with hand-embroidered monograms, the soap was white but richly perfumed. And Mike himself was present in the array of brushes and utensils that lined the shelves.

I turned on a faucet. The water pressure was pure Park Avenue; it gushed out like a break in a main. The water swirled and rose. Something was stuck in the drain. I put my finger into the drain and drew out a blob of wet hair and slugged it into the wastebasket, wiping my hands on one of the luxurious towels.

I wandered back out of the bathroom. "Biglow, did anything unusual occur the last day you saw Mr. Rawn? Anything at all?"

Biglow pursed his lips with effort. "I recall very well the whole day, Mr. Blunt. We came here after closing the old apartment. Mr. Rawn came after everything was settled here; he was the last to leave the old place. He looked through his mail here and we went through the apartment. Everything was just as he ordered it. He approved, and that was all. A few hours later he left for the theater. He told me he had a call to make; he left a bit early."

I nodded, remembering that call well, and looked about the chilly, perfect room. Suddenly I turned to face Biglow.

"Do *you* like all this, Biglow?"

His face was a quiet mask of faithfulness.

"It is quite grand, Mr. Blunt. Most suitable to Mr. Rawn's type of public life. It is necessary that he be ready to entertain a great deal. The apartment seemed completely satisfactory." There was a silence, then he went on in a more personal tone, "I hope you'll find Mr. Rawn, sir. It is most important to my personal peace of mind, if I may venture to say so, Mr. Blunt."

I patted his shoulder wordlessly. The quiet moment was broken by the buzzer. Biglow moved to the door, and I heard the boom of a deep, familiar voice.

"Well, if it isn't Sandy Blunt!" the voice entered the room like a rush of surf, bearing on it the substantial form of Inspector Dan Cassidy. "Hear tell from the cubs down at the station you're getting to be quite the writer up at your place. And Pat Curry was talking to me just this morning. Congratulations!"

"Thanks, Inspector. Got anything for the *Globe* right now? I could use a good lead on this thing."

"Oh," Cassidy spewed scorn, "one of them routine disappearances. Maybe publicity. Them theater people will do anything.. . ."

"I'm surprised at the Big Boy wasting your time, if the Main

Office thinks it's routine," I jibed.

Cassidy shrugged eloquently. "Huh! I got my orders from Headquarters, all right. Someone is interested in this Mike O'Rahn, or whatever his name is. Quite the whoop-tee-do at the Office. It's free tickets for the D. A., if you ask me!"

"Sure," I murmured.

"Did he have any big debts?" Cassidy spoke to Biglow, who stiffened.

"Mr. Rawn was a very good business man," Biglow assured the Inspector, "I know that he did not have any debts."

"Oh, Inspector," I broke in, "I suppose you want to know; Michael Rawn visited me and John Olds the afternoon of that last night. We knew him from 'way back . . .'"

The Inspector made notes in his little book. When I came to the part about Mike intimating a secret, I skipped. I saw no reason to bring up the name of Lisa Cushman. It could not matter, anyhow. Mike hadn't told me; I didn't actually know. When I finished Cassidy seemed satisfied.

"Thanks, Sandy," he slapped his notebook shut. "It's something to report, anyhow. Now, Mr. Biglow . . .'"

The phone rang, and Biglow held it out to the Inspector coldly. "For you, sir," he said precisely.

Cassidy listened for a minute, then exploded. I turned from the door on my way out.

"What is it, Inspector?"

The Inspector adjusted his hat and joined me at the door.

"I'll be seeing you later, Mr. Biglow," he called as he closed the door behind us. As we waited for the elevator he began.

"Ever hear of a woman called Martha Wain?"

"Sure, Mike's leading lady in the play. Why?"

"Well," the Inspector sighed heavily, "she's down at the station now, yelling her head off. Now *she's* missing someone! A husband, it seems, that she ain't seen since the shindig here at Rawn's apartment."

We entered the elevator.

"Last night?" I asked. "The same night as . . . "

"The same," he nodded emphatically. "Says she came here with him; but he wasn't to be found when she left and she ain't seen him since! Imagine; her own husband!"

"Martha Wain . . ." I mused. "I didn't know she was married."

"Well," the Inspector said as we reached the quiet avenue, "she wasn't telling it. Separated, they told me. But she had a husband just the same. In the play too, he was. Name of Floyd Harvey."

CHAPTER FIVE

Before the Dutch Gothic mass of gables, gargoyles, marble cornices and ironwork that was numbered 1099, was a roaming throng of newspapermen and women, some of whom I recognized. Cassidy must have spilled the story, I reasoned, for I could not believe that Biglow would be intimidated into telling Mike's business. I stood across the street and a little away, trying to plan a campaign. It stood to reason that if Lady Matilda Wintarthur had never made any attempt to see or know Mike, she was not welcoming the avalanche of publicity the people on her front steps might bring her. Plainly, she was seeing no one. I studied the front of the town house for a minute, then crossed the street and walked slowly down 83rd Street east. The Wintarthur mansion had no service entrance on Fifth Avenue, yet it was only a few doors from the 83rd Street corner. As I got halfway along the block I saw what I was looking for. A small alley led from the back of the houses that lay in the middle of the block; and the servants must use this to leave or enter. There was a padlocked gate giving onto the sidewalk, so I lit a cigarette and waited, one eye on the back of the town house of the unseen Lady Wintarthur.

Fifteen minutes later, a small door in the back of the house opened, and a stern woman looked out. I moved idly to the curb, busily searching for something in the gutter. I half-turned in time to see the stern tall woman give instructions to a young girl with a basket on her arm. The girl nodded her head impatiently, and started out the alley toward me, drawing a key from her purse as she came. I kept away from the gate and prayed that none of the newshawks would come around the corner from Fifth Avenue.

The girl locked the gate after her and swung along the sidewalk toward Madison, away from me. I followed her at a short distance. As she turned south on Madison I stepped up beside her and flashed my company smile. She had red hair, a few freckles, and a bright eye.

"Good-morning; my name is Sandy Blunt of the *New York Globe*, and this is Chivalry Week, miss. I hope you'll permit me to carry your market-basket for you?" I put out a hand.

The girl looked up at me and replied pertly, "And my name is Greta Garbo of the Nut House. Be on your way, smarty, or I'll yell for a cop."

"No, really, miss. I'm serious. I've got to do a feature story on a chivalrous deed I do today, and the earlier I do it, the sooner I'm done. Please let me carry your basket and walk along with you."

She pursed her lips, but looked my press card over. We walked for about six steps, then she laughed and looked me in the face again.

"Only an Irishman could give out such blarney so early in the morning!"

"Sure," I confessed eagerly, taking the basket, "my mother's people were all Irish. But blarney it is not."

"Well, come on then. We go over here first."

We crossed the street and entered a fruit market. I carried the basket, and took all the packages. Her name was Ann McGuire and she was a maid at Lady Wintarthur's. The cook was breaking her in; she had been there just three weeks today.

When we got back, she tried to take the basket at the iron gate, but I smiled brightly.

"Oh, Miss McGuire," I remonstrated, "I've got to carry it to the door. Please; that's part of my job!"

She hesitated, and I rushed on authoritatively, "You see, I have to ascertain the environment, the house the lady comes from. It isn't your responsibility at all, Miss McGuire."

She tossed her head, and we went through together.

"OK," she decided. "After all, it was none of my doing, your coming along; the old battleaxe can't blame me!"

"What old battleaxe? Lady Wintarthur?"

"No, not her," Ann McGuire pouted, "it's the cook, Mrs. Brewelhide. She and I don't . . . . get on, you might say." She giggled, and I took her arm in a solicitous gesture.

"I'll explain everything," I assured as we reached the kitchen.

"That you, McGuire?" came a voice of beaten brass, the minute we were through the door. "You're late!"

The tall woman I had seen from the sidewalk turned from the refrigerator across the room.

"And who might you be?" she hailed me.

"Madam," I began, "this is Chivalry Week, and it is one of my duties to help . . ."

"Help yourself right back where you came from, young man," she blared. "When we need help we go to an employment agency!"

I held my ground by the back door grimly. I was inside now,

and meant to stay if I possibly could.

"Madam," I declaimed, "you misunderstand my mission . . ."

"I understand you're a snooper, and I'll have no more of you! Get out before I call the police!"

She glared at me with deep scorn. A butler entered through a swinging door.

"Mrs. Brewelhide, contain yourself," he interrupted. "Madam will hear you in the breakfast room. Who are you, sir, and what is your business here?" he asked me, as Mrs. Brewelhide, at the stove now, glared at Ann McGuire.

"It's Chivalry Week . . ." Ann apologized lamely, and I bolstered her excuses.

"I was performing my duty in coming here with Miss McGuire," I stated. "She has no responsibility for my presence." I drew out my press card again. "I'm a feature writer for the *New York Globe* . . ."

"A newspaperman; one of *them!*" Mrs. Brewelhide erupted.

"I must ask you to leave at once," the butler said firmly.

I held my ground. "I must see the lady of the house to affirm my conclusions and to complete my story of the deed of chivalry I must write about . . . helping Miss McGuire. I must have an affidavit from the employer," I went on, gathering momentum.

"I am sorry . . ." the butler began, while Mrs. Brewelhide shouted above him, "Nonsense, every bit of it . . ."

Just then the door swung open. All talk ceased as we whirled around to face the alabaster-ebony woman in the doorway, quiet and commanding. I knew I was looking at Lady Matilda Wintarthur.

She was very small, very pale, and dressed in sweeping black, with a lace shawl over her shoulders. In her hand was a thin ebony stick with a gold head. Her hair was white and piled high on her head. She stood there like some small knowing bird, seeing us all with a glance at once bright and impersonal.

"What is this uproar, Buckram?" she asked the butler peremptorily.

"I . . ." he started, but I broke in.

"Lady Wintarthür, I am Sandy Blunt, of the *New York Globe.* I'm hunting for Michael Rawn." I had hoped it would make an impression, and it did. There was utter silence for a moment.

"Come in and have breakfast with me, young man," Lady Wintarthur said, and turned away. I followed her through the door, through a pantry, and into the front of the house. We were in the basement, with small high windows on the Avenue, and one glance showed me the restless feet of the horde of curious reporters outside.

"Sit down," came my hostess' voice as I looked about me. The room was small and beautifully furnished. A fire burned in a small fireplace, shedding an amber light over the priceless carpet, a gilding on the silver service. The room was a museum piece, every appointment a treasure. With a flickering thought I wondered if Lady Matilda Wintarthur could in any way be connected with Mike's sudden, overwhelming affluence.

"Coffee?" inquired the bird-like figure as I took a place across from her. I nodded, and she poured me a cup and went on directly, "What do you want to know? I warn you that this intrusion of my privacy is not taken kindly by me, but I dare say it is the quickest way of disposing of you."

I could see that Chivalry Week had quietly died on its way out of the kitchen, so I came to the point at once.

"I'm Michael Rawn's best friend . . ." I began, but she broke in, coldly.

"I am not interested in your status, young man. I am tired of being disturbed. I am prepared, since you have seen fit to invade my privacy in this manner, to talk to you. If you disturb me any further than this I shall require police protection. Do you understand?"

I nodded. Her face was cruel, cold; yet somehow I had the idea she was protecting herself as much from her thoughts and her memories as against any physical contact with the outside world.

"I would like to know whether or not you can tell me anything to help me in my search for your missing grand-nephew," I said quietly.

For a long minute Lady Matilda Wintarthur looked at me unwaveringly. When she spoke her voice was softer.

"I cannot say that I can help. I have never set eyes on my grand-nephew. I have never seen the boy you call Michael Rawn."

"He listed your name as . . ."

"So I understand," she interrupted. "I am his last legal relative. But I did not know him. I do not mean to, ever."

I studied the old figure, stern and disciplined in her black silk and lace. I sensed a story; a reason for her last sentence. It was not merely circumstance that had never brought Lady Matilda Wintarthur and Michael Rawn face to face.

"I need to know anything pertinent to Michael Rawn's disappearance, Lady Wintarthur," I began, "because even though I was his

34

friend, I knew very little about Mike. Is there any particular reason why you didn't know Mike? Something ·that stood between you?"

"I shall speak frankly with you, provided I am not bothered again." She pressed hypnotic eyes into mine and I nodded. She put her coffee cup down slowly, and her voice began cautiously, as though repeating thoughts long buried, thoughts Lady Matilda Wintarthur had no wish to disturb.

"I have every reason for not knowing the young man you call Michael Rawn. I will tell you, Mr. Blunt, the whole story. It goes back a bit . . . it goes back a long time." Her voice faltered; she took a deep breath and resumed. "My late husband and I reared Michael's mother. She was my niece. Her name was Alice; my sister had left her in my care at her own death. My husband and I doted on Alice. We gave her everything; we loved her dearly. On a business trip to Ohio my husband took us both along. Alice was a lovely girl of eighteen. One day we toured several mines; Alice met a young man. I never understood how, for he was unlike anyone she had ever known. A miner, very rough and poor, but she ran away with him—we could do nothing with her. My husband and I never forgave him, for she was young and infatuated. Their first child was a boy . . ."

She stopped, and I held my breath. Then her voice went on, dreaming, living her old memories once again.

"Then there was a little girl. About that time I learned from Alice, who wrote to me, that her husband was jealous of her, of the niceties she tried to instill into her children. He drank; abused her terribly. I urged her to divorce him, to return to us; but Alice would not leave her home. I felt sick beyond words for her, but her will to stay with . . . with that man, put her outside our help." Once again Lady Wintarthur stopped; her voice dropped to a whisper. "Then it came. The scandal. We never saw Alice again. We put her out of our thoughts / . ."

There was an unearthly quiet in the room. I stared at her, a figure out of another age. Her voice was toneless, her eyes vacant as she went on, ". . . Ten years . . . ten long years . . . a lifetime . . ." Her eyes swept my face unseeingly. "And you wonder that I never saw him—that I could never look on the face of Michael Lasker . . .?"

She stared into the fire, and suddenly a tear fell like glittering ice down her graven face. I was puzzled and shocked! Something was very wrong with my calculations. Lasker! I was Mike's oldest friend and the name Lasker meant nothing to me. Like skittering bats the double nature of the disappearance darted through my brain. Ten years! I looked down at Lady Matilda Wintarthur. She had not moved and was staring now into the fire. Quietly I turned and made my way back to the kitchen.

"Thanks, Ann," I called as I passed through the kitchen on my way out. She smiled and Mrs. Brewelhide snorted loudly. I went out the alley into 83rd Street.

Walking down Madison Avenue I breathed deeply. Curry had been right about the next of kin providing a lead. There had been something in the past of Michael Rawn which had caused conventional Lady Wintarthur to shrink from any contact. Michael *Rawn?* She had said Michael Lasker. She had said "the boy you call Michael Rawn . . ." Mike had changed his name! Something in his life, before even I had known him, had caused him to hide his identity.

I decided the next step would be to go over all the old newspapers in the *Globe* library of ten years ago. It would mean considerable work, but the time was definite, at least. I knew it was useless to try to press Lady Wintarthur for more detail. I would have to discover it on my own.

As I crossed the corner at Third and 42nd a large car drew up beside me, slowed to keep pace with me across the street. As I reached the curb I glanced curiously up at it. The curtains were drawn, giving it the withdrawn air of a huge hearse. I smiled at my thought as I whirled through the revolving door of the Automat; and once inside, went for a second look to the big window that made the whole front of the restaurant a goldfish bowl. I was surprised at what I saw.

The big car had stopped, and the driver was talking over his shoulder to someone in the rear, safely curtained from my sight. Somehow I had the overwhelming conviction that the car and its mysterious occupant had followed me. I leaped back into the revolving door, and was spit out onto the curb. As I started out toward the car it leaped forward like a spurred horse, up the grade of 42nd Street in the direction of Tudor City. I stared after it, baffled and somewhat angry. I knew I had been right. I was being watched. And I had no way of knowing how far the car had followed me. With a sudden rush of anger, I saw the limousine turn north on Second Avenue. I went back into the Automat and got a tray of food.

I was nearly finished when John Olds came in, looked around aimlessly until he saw my raised hand. He signaled me to wait, and brought his tray back and sat down.

36

"I'm through for the day," he announced, "but I didn't want to go to my painting lesson until I'd seen you. I hoped you'd be here. What's new?"

I told Johnnie about Lady Matilda Wintarthur. "I'm going up to the library now, to go over the ten-year-old newspapers—try to see if I can't find out just what happened between Mike's family and the old folks."

Johnnie whistled. "It's a wonder Mike didn't say something; a peeress for a great-aunt!"

"Mike was quite a boy," I remarked, "in lots of ways."

Suddenly Johnnie looked over at me. "Say Sandy, would you mind if I came along with you? I can afford to lose one lesson; the brushes will keep. And you may need some help. OK?"

"Sure. I will need help. I don't know how many papers I'll have to look over; I don't even know whether I'll find anything at all!"

As we walked up the sidewalk toward the Globe Building, John demanded, "What do you really think has happened to Mike? How about the show?"

"I honest to God don't have any idea what's happened to Mike," I told Johnnie. "Cushman will probably have to close his show."

"That understudy is all over the latest editions," John went on. "You suppose the two disappearances connect?"

"They must tie together somehow," I frowned. "It's logical." I told Johnnie about the short-haired blond man I had mistaken for Mike at the party. John whistled again.

"You must have been the last person who saw Floyd Harvey . . ."

I shook my head. "Keep it under your hat. Dan Cassidy is assigned to the case. I don't want him running all over *my* beat."

"Cassidy's been all over the place already," John informed me. "He was up to talk to me in the office today. I told him about Mike's visit to us, but that's all." After a pause, he went on casually, "I . . . didn't mention anything about . . . Miss Cushman . . . or that Mike had said anything about a secret."

Our eyes caught and we smiled silently.

As we stepped out of the elevator, John spoke again. "Oh, Sandy, before I forget. Pat Curry went home a little while ago; he gave me a message for you. Someone, some man, called for you. Name of Valerian. Didn't leave a number or anything. Said he'd call again."

I swore under my breath as I thanked John Olds. This was the second call. I wasn't so damned hard to reach. I was positive that

I knew no one at all with the name Valerian.

As John and I took off our coats in the old news library, I dismissed the name and the phone calls from my mind. We had work to do, and it might take a deadly long time, and be fruitless at that.

I realize now how much luck entered into our work that night. We started in the afternoon, and searched papers for four hours without let-up. We read everything in the library of ten-year-old news features, going backwards through the files. The day force went off, and one by one the night force came grumpily to work. At nine we had found nothing and seemed to have read reams of news, yet covered a pitifully small number of papers. At nine John went out and returned with doughnuts and coffee. We smoked and rested.

"We've got to work out some system," Johnnie sighed at last. "I've hunted for Michael Rawn, or Michael Lasker, whichever it would be." Anyhow, we'll never get through, reading every item as we go!"

I had told Johnnie about Lady Matilda Wintarthur's mention of the name Lasker; presumably it was Michael's real name. Johnnie had greeted the revelation with non-committal silence. I wondered if he were wanting to help for Mike's sake, or for his own curiosity, but I said nothing about it.

"How's this?" I asked. "You take odd months; I'll take even. We'll read the headlines. That gives us six months apiece for the year. Maybe we can find it that way. It'll go faster, that's certain."

He agreed, and we put out our cigarettes and returned to the task. For the first hour or so we stopped from time to time to discuss old stories, some we had known, some we envied for the way they were written. As the night wore on we worked silently, quickly, relentlessly, combing every paper with hard, eager eyes burning from the shifting clouds of tobacco smoke that came from the hard-working night force. Silence crept over us like a pall.

It was three A. M. when Johnnie's head slid to his arms. I looked over at him and smiled, doggedly getting down another paper. It would be the last for tonight. John had to go back to the grind tomorrow, and he had lost one night of his precious painting as it was.

Sleepily I flipped open the first page, thinking how far away and blessed the apartment and bed seemed, when my eyes caught on the paper like wool on burrs.

"Johnnie!"

He jerked awake at my voice, came to look over my shoulder. Together we stared at the second page headline.

MINOR FREED IN TRIPLE TRAGEDY

Dumbly my eyes met John's. When I spoke my lips were stiff. "Get me a couple issues before this. This would be the end of it."

Wordlessly he deposited three papers before me and we read. All at once a chill flew up my spine to the base of my skull. "Look . . ." I put my finger down on the top of the papers, pointing to the date when the story had first hit the papers.

"My God . . ." Johnnie's voice was hoarse.

The date was Wednesday, the 27th. The month was October.

CHAPTER SIX

It was quite a story. At fourteen Michael had been tried for murder. No wonder he had not talked about his past. Mike had been trying for a long time to forget.

The newspaper stories were explicit. His parents had quarrelled often. An inveterate alcoholic, his father had overridden Mike's mother, a quiet, well-bred woman, drained to nondescript opacity at thirty. The sister had been anaemic, constantly in the care of visiting nurses when the father didn't forcibly interfere. So ran the testimony. A neighbor had testified to a terrible row one night, and the next morning a fellow miner had found the Laskers strewn about their squalid frame house unconscious. The sister and father were dead—the mother died on the way to a hospital. Only the young son, Michael, survived.

Then, the newspapers boldly hinted, politics had entered the case of young Michael Lasker. Elections were imminent; an ambitious young prosecutor named Denton had led Michael, young and frightened, to the stand—accused of murder! He had fainted. The story had become a sensation. *Globe* writers whose names I had learned to revere began to appear in the by-lines.

Mike's testimony had been simple. His father had brought home liquor—had insisted they all drink with him. They had, out of fear of his terrible temper. The drink had been illicit, bootleg gin, investigation showed. That was all. The fading newspaper pictures underlined Mike and the experience. His face was tragic and quiet—sick. As the case had attracted the bigger papers, they took up the cudgel and belabored the local government without mercy. Denton, the prosecutor, was thoroughly flayed; the elections turned into a rout. The jury took ten minutes to bring in its acquittal verdict and Michael was made a ward of the County until he should go to college, for which purpose an unknown socialite had established a trust fund in Michael's name. There it ended. We knew about Mike's youth and about his talent for silence. It must have been then that Mike changed his name, leaving his tragic past buried behind him when I had first met him.

"My God," John Olds said slowly.

There was a long quiet between us. I wondered dully what connection, what ghost out of the past had come to Michael on the night of his great fulfillment—what surprise so unwelcome as to force him from his lighted path. Of one thing I felt almost certain. The trial and Mike's present disappearance were linked. But outside of Johnnie and myself, there was only Lady Matilda Wintarthur who knew anything of Mike's personality in relation to his background. And she had firmly closed me out. It was checkmate.

We replaced the newspapers and took a cab home. In the kitchen Johnnie and I sat in our pyjamas for a while, drinking milk, unable to voice the thoughts that filled our minds. John broke the silence.

"What will you do now?"

"I don't know. I think I'll go back to Mike's apartment tomorrow; maybe talk to Martha Wain. Somewhere in Mike's place there must be a story, a connection. And Martha Wain ought to be able to tell me something. She went with Mike for a while, before he met Lisa. And I'd like to talk to her about her husband, Floyd Harvey."

"Do you think the two disappearances tie together, Sandy?"

"Hell," I spoke roughly, "I don't know. Harvey might be out on one of those extra-marital sessions somewhere."

We ambled into the studio room and got into bed. "Don't wake me when you go," I instructed. "I'll decide what to do when I get up. But I think I'll skip over to Mike's first. I'd like to go over that apartment completely."

John punched out the light near his bed and was snoring gently in ten minutes. I lay awake for some time, a single thought going round and round in my mind like the tigers around the tree in *Little Black Sambo*. Valerian! He had phoned me twice. I fretted to sleep thinking of the tigers chasing the name Valerian around and around the tree.

When I woke it was late afternoon, and I hurried to dress after my bath. I got Martha Wain's address from the girl at the switchboard at Cushman Productions, and phoned her.

"Miss Wain, this is Mr. Blunt. I wonder if I might come over to talk to you sometime this evening?"'

There was a moment's hesitation before she replied. "Why, yes, I guess it's all right. What did you want to talk to me about?"

"About Mr. Rawn's disappearance; as well as your husband's. I'm on a feature story, and feel you might help me. All right?"

She paused uncertainly, then said indefinitely, "I guess so. I don't see what I can help with though. Come about nine, I guess."

I hung up thoughtfully, and went up to the corner of West End Avenue for a cab. I gave the driver Michael Rawn's Park Avenue address.

I was certain Mike Rawn had not vanished of his own free will. And there I had the handle to the difficulty of a New York disappearance. People came from everywhere to trade their talent or their goods, and went; leaving no trace on a city that is a shifting monument to the work of a million souls. It came to me that a disappearance is never quite a fact—no one *knows* what has happened. Working on a disappearance is working on a presumption. You dare not presume too much, lest in the middle of your search the missing one comes blithely back, with a logical excuse to make you foolish, if not prying.

But I had my assignment, my story was growing. I felt my natural high feelings seep back; I drew a deep breath as the cab crept to the curb under the marquee. I had a start on my story and Mike would know I had not meant to pry.

From the doorman I learned that Biglow had gone out, but had left a key for me in case I should happen to arrive during his absence. I frowned as the elevator lifted me to the penthouse, and as I stepped out I thought the operator gave me a strange smile. I turned, puzzled, but the doors closed chastely in my face.

I entered the penthouse and turned on a light, walking through the living room directly to the library. It was a small cosy room, still modern for all the books, but without the grandiose spaces that robbed the living room of simple humanity. The shelves covered the walls and were full, and I wondered how Mike had accumulated so many volumes so quickly. On a desk in the center of the room was an ivory and silver desk set, richly carved and chased. A box of letter paper, with MICHAEL RAWN in strong Roman engraving across the top of the sheets, stared up at me. Everything was religiously in its place.

I ambled into the living room, turning on lamps as I went. Lastly I snapped the indirect lighting on at the wall, and looked at the portrait of Michael.

The background seemed to be a dark rising hill, dimly visible. The clouded dull sky held a moon, faintly gleaming, and across the top of the picture the lowering clouds cast a thick, masking, grey nimbus. Away from this ground stood the figure of Michael, thin and spirited, dynamic. He wore dark trousers which seemed almost to match the earth on which he stood; his face rose pale and stark out of a dark, long-sleeved shirt. One hand held something that looked like an apple, except that it was perfectly round, like an orange. I looked steadily at the face, and as always a feeling of uneasy disloyalty swept over me, an uncanny feeling of uncomfortable embarrassment. Yet it was the face of my friend—the dark reddish hair, the wide high brow, the cheekbones and the narrow jaw, that expression of eagerness, almost grimness in repose. There was something of a smile on Michael's lips, yet the expression was not completely pleasant—it was impelling, and at the same time inscrutible, possessed; just short of mocking. The eyes were large and handsome; the brows were Michael's broad, aristocratic sweeps. It was a truly magnificent picture; it was Michael Rawn, the Success. And knowing Mike, I loathed the picture with the deepest fibre within me. Aggravated, I moved deliberately closer. And received a shock.

The thing Michael Rawn held in his hand was dark, bloody red and spherical; but it was no orange for all its shape. It was a small, minutely painted globe of the world. At such close range, I instinctively looked at the small engraved metal tag at the bottom of the frame. What I read made my heart beat faster. *Michael Rawn and the World,* it read, and under it was the artist's name. The name was Demos Valerian.

There was a sudden slight rustling behind me and I whirled. The name Valerian had put me on edge, and I expelled a deep breath as I saw Lisa Cushman leisurely coming down the wide stairs. With sudden dawning I understood the elevator boy's smile. I strode to her, and she smiled. She had startled me and she knew it.

"You like it?" She indicated the portrait.

"No." My answer was almost sullen. "It isn't like Mike at all. If you asked me, I'd say the artist had it in for Mike."

She laughed. "You're wrong. Mr. Valerian is a good friend of Mike's. I never liked the picture myself, but Mike was crazy about it."

I looked at her as we sat down on the sofa. She was wearing a plain black dress, black shoes and gloves and a hat, a fur coat and small pearls in her ears. Her hair was caught up in one of those hanging nets.

I wanted to touch it. I sat as close to her as I dared, lighting her cigarette as we started to smoke.

"Do you come here often?" I opened.

"No." She hesitated the barest moment. "I just came here today to see if there was anything I could do." She smiled at me. "I have my own key," she went on directly. I looked down. After a pause she said suddenly, "Are you working with the police?"

"Not a bit." I looked at her. A tiny frown wrinkled her forehead. "I'm on my own. Inspector Cassidy is on the case. He's a bit of a friend of mine, but I'm playing a lone hand."

For some reason she seemed reassured. At last she said, "Have you discovered anything?"

I shook my head wearily. "Nothing."

"Could I help in any way?" she asked.

"Not that I know of."

Suddenly she leaned toward me urgently. "Sandy, you've *got* to find Mike. You've got to find him right away!"

I looked at her with some surprise. She turned her head away and said in a lower tone, "It's so . . . inexplicable . . . his going away. It's so . . . well," she smiled, "I guess I'm excited too much."

I looked up at the big portrait above us.

"I'd like to know about the man who painted that picture," I mused. She seemed glad of a diversion.

"Mr. Valerian? Well, I have met him several times; I don't know much about him. He has a great deal of money, no business that any one knows about; he seems retired. Mr. Valerian is a very accomplished artist, but he doesn't have to paint for money and won't paint anyone he doesn't choose to paint."

"I suppose his not having to paint is what made Mike like this picture," I judged.

"I don't think so," Lisa laughed. "Mr. Valerian painted Michael almost the minute he saw him—said he was the perfect subject. They got on very well together, from all I know."

We studied the great portrait for a long minute, then I said, "It's not a comfortable picture."

"No." After another pause, Lisa asked quietly, "You liked Mike a lot, Sandy?"

I nodded. It occurred to me that I liked Mike a lot and she loved him. Which is why neither of us liked the portrait that seemed to us both to be so superficially Michael Rawn.

"Mike was my best friend," I went on, "and more than that. He was clever and wise and good." I struck my hands together. "I wish I could do something beside sit and talk about him. But he's gone without a sign; I don't even know anyone who knew him here, outside of John Olds and myself and you. Your father couldn't help me, either."

"I didn't know Michael too well myself," Lisa mused, and I turned to face her.

"Tell me about the first time you saw him," I requested.

She recollected a minute, then began.

"It was at my father's office, about seven months ago. I was shopping and dropped in on him. Michael was there. He wasn't exactly attractive, but—fascinating. His hair gleamed because he was sitting with the light behind him as I came through the door. Father introduced us and Michael got up to shake my hand. I knew why father had decided to star him in his first play. Michael *was* a star, the kind that is born knowing everything he must know. I went to some of Michael's rehearsals. He was amazing to watch; the way he learned from others. He was utterly without vanity where learning was concerned. Once told, Michael had learned forever."

As her story halted, I looked at her. She was lovely. Her face grew thoughtful as she went on. "Michael Rawn was simply born to greatness. He asked me to lunch a few times. Father didn't seem to approve at first, but then one day father spoke to me about Michael. Father told me he was going to be a great man, that if Mike asked me, it might be well to think seriously of him as . . . as my husband. Shortly after that, Michael did propose. I—well, I told him I would like to think it over. The next day he sent me a ring; and I wore it. I supposed I was in love with Michael. He was always wonderfully kind and considerate."

Abruptly I broke in, "You don't seem to be the sort of girl who wouldn't know when she was in love." For a moment she looked at me directly, a mystified expression on her face. She went on quietly.

"I knew soon enough. Father seemed pleased, and Michael was. I thought—well, actually I never got to know Michael really well." She took a sudden deep breath. "It's just since he's gone that I feel I'm coming to know him, if you can understand that."

A long silence fell between us; I wanted to keep her there talking, so I questioned, "Maybe you knew someone else who knew Mike— someone I could talk to."

All at once Lisa's voice stiffened, her next words dropping like marbles on cement. "A lot of people knew Mike better than I did," she remarked grimly. "Martha Wain. Talk to her, Sandy. Martha knew Mike well. And Mr. Valerian. And Jasmine Le Valley." She rose, and her eyes on my face were cold. "Go to them. Ask them how they first met Michael Rawn. Any of them ought to have quite a story to tell you." She looked at me as though I were a blundering fool, which I felt; and without another word walked away. In the doorway she met Biglow, coming in. She thanked him for holding the door open, and left. I stood staring after her, wondering what I had done to set off the outburst of freezing sparks.

Biglow greeted me, and brought me a drink. As I lifted it I noticed he was standing before me, and I looked up.

"Something you want to tell me, Biglow?"

"Well, Mr. Blunt," he went on carefully, "you asked me yesterday if I recalled anything that seemed the least out of the way, anything that happened on the day Mr. Rawn moved into this apartment."

"Yes?"

"Well, this; Mr. Blunt. After we had moved in, Mr. Rawn sent me downtown to a cutlery store, to get a pair of scissors. I remember them very well. Razor steel, he asked for, and they were hard to get, but finally I located them in a store on Lexington Avenue."

"What about them, Biglow?"

"They're gone, Mr. Blunt," his voice was troubled. "I know they're gone. I left them in the library as I was told, but they're not there. I can't find the scissors anywhere. They've disappeared."

"They weren't in his make-up box?"

"No, sir. It's at the theater. They aren't anywhere at all."

I rose. "Biglow, I'd like to look at Mr. Rawn's papers again, if you don't mind helping me."

He hesitated a minute, then led me up the stairs and into the bedroom. While he worked the dial of the safe, I looked into the bathroom. It occurred to me that all this galaxy of brushes, powder—new, had never been used. Mike was thrifty in his way, and as I returned to find Biglow placing Mike's papers on the writing desk, I asked him, "Biglow, what did you and Mr. Rawn do with all the toilet articles from the old apartment?"

He looked up in surprise. "We threw them out, Mr. Blunt. Mr. Rawn had me go out and buy everything new. The best. It was quite a long list. He said he wanted everything in the new place to be as new as the life he was beginning."

I nodded, but asked him the name of the superintendent of the old apartment house. Mr. Horace Jennings. I wrote it down, and began to look over the small bunch of items that comprised Mike's personal papers. My quick inventory gave me a shock.

"Is this everything that was in the safe, Biglow?"

"Yes, Mr. Blunt. Everything is there on the desk."

"Except the bundle of old letters, Biglow."

Puzzled, he came over to the desk. Aghast, he repeated my exclamation, "Yes, sir . . . except the old letters."

"Biglow," I urged, "do you know what they were?"

Biglow was obviously worried.

"Mr. Blunt, I did wrong," he mourned. "I do not know what they contained, but they were most important. Mr. Rawn held them up to show them to me one day almost a year ago. 'Biglow,' he said, 'if anything ever happens to me, you take these and hide them at once.' I ought to have removed them as he ordered me."

Biglow's worry began to infect me. For the first time a feeling of definite personal intent, of movement beyond my own, came to me. Someone else was interested in Mike and his disappearance. I seized Biglow's thin shoulders.

"Those letters, Biglow. Who wrote them? Who would want them?" In a flash of remembrance I recalled Lisa's black bag, the bag she had not let out of her hands during our conversation. "Were they Miss Cushman's letters?"

Biglow's reply was frightened, but very definite.

"I don't know what they were, Mr. Blunt. But they couldn't have been from Miss Cushman. They're much too old."

CHAPTER SEVEN

When I finally left Mike's apartment, I phoned Martha Wain, to ask if I could drop over then to see her. But she put me off, and asked me if I could come up the next day, which was Sunday, October 31. I said I could, and she made a little joke about her first free Saturday in some time, and mentioned having a big date.

In the light of later events, I knew that had I gone to see her, even over her protests, the mystery of Michael Rawn would have ended that night. But hindsight is always easy.

As it was, the next morning was a lovely Sunday, and as I made my way to Mike's old apartment, I walked along whistling. I had turned in the second episode of my story, and Pat Curry liked it, even believed that it was increasing circulation.

I had planned a busy enough day. I meant to contact my phoning friend, Mr. Valerian. He was in the directory and I had written his number in my little book. I wanted to see Mike's old apartment, not for any particular clue, but simply for what it might tell me. I wanted to talk to one Jasmine Le Valley, whoever she might be. Then I would go to see Martha Wain in the evening.

Horace Jennings, the superintendent of Mike's former apartment house, was a large negro of commanding presence and a handsome voice. He remembered Michael Rawn very well.

"I'd be most glad to have you look into Mr. Rawn's apartment, Mr. Blunt," he informed me, "except that it was rented the very day Mr. Rawn moved out. It would be outside my personal authority to open the apartment."

"That's all right, Mr. Jennings, and thank you," I gave in, slightly disappointed. "Did Mr. Rawn leave anything behind?"

He nodded pleasantly and led me into the basement, pointing to two bushel baskets neatly placed beside a service door.

"That is everything, just as Mr. Rawn had me get it from his apartment the day he left. I'd be happy to have you look at it, Mr. Blunt. I was sorry to hear of Mr. Rawn's disappearance. I trust nothing of a calamitous nature has occurred."

"This is everything, Mr. Jennings?"

He nodded his head emphatically. "Yes sir. I brought those baskets down here myself, and put them there where you see them. They haven't been touched at all."

I thanked him again and bent to inspect the contents.

Six pairs of shoes, the hand-made shoes Mike had always promised himself; that I knew he never would have resoled. He had talked of such a luxury in school. Mike was thrifty, but when he had a whim, it was a costly one. There was a pile of magazines; *The Writer, Colliers, Saturday Evening Post, Life, Time.* A few old letters, from agents, from a lawyer, bills marked paid. Old coat hangers, a wool scarf I recognized from school, three gloves, all without mates. Mike had been passionately fond of fine leather. The small gloves with their long fingers suddenly brought Mike back in an overwhelming surge of recognition. I put the contents of the baskets slowly back as I had found them. One thought rose to the surface with the significance of oil on an ocean. The one thing I ought to have found was not there.

"Mr. Jennings," I called, "did Mr. Rawn leave anything at all in the apartment beside this stuff in the baskets?"

"No, sir," Jennings said firmly, "Mr. Rawn was neat as a pin. He packed all that stuff, and once I got it out there wasn't another bit."

Thoughtfully, I thanked him for his cooperation and walked into the clear October air. I had learned little, but what I had learned was positive enough. And it worried me unaccountably.

There were no old brushes in either of the bushel baskets of Mike's trash, yet Biglow had said Mike had thrown them all out; that he had been sent to buy a complete set of toilet articles for Mike.

And within the last twenty-four hours, someone with a key and the combination of Mike's wall-safe, had stolen the packet of old letters Mike had said were very important to him.

I walked, deep in thought, over to Broadway to my favorite restaurant, the C. and L., and ordered my lunch. After my Manhattan, I went to the phone and called the number of Mr. Demos Valerian, an address on Riverside Drive. A smooth male voice answered.

"Hello?"

"This is Sandy Blunt, of the *New York Globe*. Mr. Valerian has been trying to get in touch with me."

The voice was kindly incredulous. "I'm sorry, Mr. Blunt, but Mr. Valerian is out of town. For about one month. I will inform him that you called."

Almost before I realized it, the voice had hung up. I stood there and swore for a minute. Maybe it was wishful thinking, but I could have sworn the man was a liar. I studied the book again, and called a number in the Bronx.

A familiar voice called, "This is Kay McGonigle; hello! Is that you, Jim?"

I laughed. "Sorry, Miss McGonigle; this is Mr. Sandy Blunt. Remember?"

"Why, certainly, Mr. Blunt! How are things going?"

"Not too well, Miss McGonigle. That's why I phoned. I wonder if you could give me some information?"

"Anything I can help with, Mr. Blunt; I'd be too glad . . ."

"Fine, and thanks. Have you ever heard the name Jasmine Le Valley, Miss McGonigle?"

"Why, sure! Certainly, Mr. Blunt—of course; *everyone* knows Jazzy!"

"Where could I find her?"

"At the Rose Palace, Mr. Blunt. Jasmine Le Valley is her stage name. Jazzy is a burlesque star. She ought to be working today. The Rose Palace is west of Times Square on 42nd Street—you can find it easy. And Jazzy is grand; she'll do anything she can to help. How did you get her name, anyhow?"

"I was told she might help me," I replied ambiguously. "Did she know Michael Rawn that you know of, Miss McGonigle?"

"It might be," Miss McGonigle thought. "Of course Mr. Rawn was a very high type artist, but in the theater you never can tell! I know Jazzy was an old friend of Mr. Cushman's—that's how I know her. She used to come up to the office sometimes."

I thanked her and went thoughtfully back to my dinner. I wondered what Michael and a burlesque queen could have in common. My meal was good, and I lingered over it, trying to piece together the little bits of information I had collected. As I recalled the incidents—the particulars I knew—one factor stood out. Everything I knew was of a negative nature. The letters stolen, the missing brushes, the vanished scissors—all I knew were the things that had gone out of my sight or away from my hand and they merely complicated my search for Mike himself. I aimlessly thought how easy it would have been had he left some cryptic message or another; anything that could have been traced. It was clear that there would be no use to try to find the man from whom Mike or Biglow had bought brushes; it would be to no purpose. The letters were known to Biglow well, but only by sight; it was more than likely that only Mike himself had known what they contained. I caught myself as I thought this last. There was someone else who must know about the scissors, the brushes, and the letters—*the person who had taken them!*

The theater called the ROSE PALACE, Burlesque Four Times Daily, was festooned with cardboard roses in apoplectic colors, and prominently displayed was a coy picture of a smiling woman with streaming blond hair. Under the picture was the motto *JASMINE (Swivel-Hips) LE VALLEY*. I walked past the theater till I came to a small alley that ran toward the back of the theater. A worn sign, painted on rusted metal, instructed . . . . *age Entrance In Rear.*

I walked to the stage door and presented my press card to the ancient male dragon who challenged me.

"Newspaper for Miss Le Valley," he yelled at no one in particular, then said to me, "Next to the last door on the right," and I went briskly through the haunted realm of backstage ghosts. Near the proscenium arch was a door with a tarnished silver star and the name Jasmine Le Valley. Both looked as though they had been there a long time. I knocked, watching a weighty blond in beads and fur stooging for a man in baggy pants on stage.

"Come on in, you big bum . . ." a whisky alto called from inside, and I opened up and stepped in.

I found myself looking at the back of a meaty female whose miraculously colored hair resembled shredded carrot with overtones of fresh strawberry. The apparition caught my reflection in the mirror and turned.

"How do you do; I'm sorry," she cried, heartily; "I thought you was the call-boy with my sandwich. Who are you?"

She stood before me in coq feathers and bugle beads and high-heeled shoes, poised and highly perfumed.

"I'm Sandy Blunt, a newspaperman, Miss Le Valley. A friend of Michael Rawn. I'd like to know if there's anything you could tell me. I'm working on his disappearance."

"Working with the bulls?" she demanded, directly.

"No; I'm on my own."

"All right, then," she announced in a friendly tone, "I ain't got nothing against the bulls themselves, see; but I just want to know who I'm talking to, that's all. Now, what's the dope?"

"That's what I don't know," I told her. "I'm looking for anyone who can tell me the least thing about Mike. Had you known him for very long?"

"Hell, no," she replied cheerfully, "but we was good friends at that, I guess." She strode up and down her dressing room, and returned to her stance before me. "He was a good kid," she decided, her bright blue eyes putting a period to her announcement.

"How did you meet Mike Rawn?" I asked.

She paused a long minute and subjected me to sharp scrutiny.

"Well," Jasmine Le Valley began, with the air of imparting the unbelievable, "maybe it ain't much of a big thing I got to tell you. It ain't maybe nothing at all. But me and the kid was very close, in a manner of speaking. I know Mike almost a year now. Frankly, it ain't a relationship that many in my business would understand; but me and Michael Rawn was collaborators, see?"

"Collaborators?"

"Sure. His own word. That's how I know. When Field Daisy

Richmond, that dancer, wrote up her memories a couple years ago, and they sold so good, she made lots of money. Well, Michael Rawn came down here one day and said if I would tell him my life history, he would write it up into a book, too, see? We been friends ever since."

"Go on, Miss Le Valley," I urged.

"Well, that's all! We worked on it; anyway, he did. But we didn't get to it, with his play and then him disappearing and all."

"How much did you and Mike do? Could I see some of it?"

"Oh, we didn't do no writing. But Michael Rawn worked on it. He was out to my mother's lots of times. I keep her in a little house out in Flatbush, and he went over there for background, he said, see? I'd go out for dinner between shows; they got as chummy as a basket of chips. The kid got to helping her around the house and all. Imagine; a big star like him! But it *is* nice out at mom's, and he said he never had much of a chance to just be around a house in the country."

I nodded. I had a picture of Mike, doing what he had always wanted to do. He had said at school that his deepest ambition was a little house in the country.

Jasmine Le Valley ruminated, "He was sure at home with mom, and she's fussy about my friends. Don't like some of them at all. But the kid was all right with her; she liked him. He used to help her empty the trash, even, and burn the papers and scrub the kitchen lino-leum and feed the chickens. He was a real guy; see?"

I agreed that I saw. "Did you originally come from Flatbush, Miss Le Valley?"

"Hell, no! I'm from a little jerkwater town in Ohio!"

I caught at that. Ohio, Mike's state! "Did you and Mike know anyone; have a friend in common, someone you both knew?"

"Sure we did," Jasmine laughed. "That's how Michael Rawn got my name in the first place! Why, I bet Sam Cushman was my first crush in this town. I knew him when he was getting his start in New York; when he didn't have a nickel in his jeans. Know anyone, say!"

The call-boy knocked, and Miss Le Valley gave him some change and garnered a sandwich, which she took to her dressing table. I rose to go, thanking her.

"Think nothing of it, chum," she waved an airy hand, "any time at all. And let me hear about the kid. He was a right guy. The bulls ought to take better care of people, anyway," she maintained.

The afternoon had thickened into early evening as I left the theater, and I felt tired. I determined to go back to our apartment until it was time for me to go to see Martha Wain. As I stumped up the last flight of stairs to our apartment, John threw open the door and called to me.

"Sandy?" His voice was sharply questioning, and I hurried.

"Yes. What is it?"

His voice poured out before I was into the studio room. "Where the hell have you been? I've been trying to get you ever since I got home! Martha Wain has called twice, and ..."

I groaned. "... and she doesn't want to see me tonight, either..."

He grabbed my arm as I got to the door. "God, no! She called in here hunting you. Call her right away. She said she knows what happened to Mike!"

"*What did you say?*" I flung myself on the phone. I got a busy signal and put the instrument down. Just as I did, it rang.

I picked it up, said "Hello."

There was a slight pause, then a husky voice, a woman's voice, said quietly, urgently, "You'd better come right ...." then a long, quiet moan. A short rattle, then a snap, and I felt I was holding a dead wire. I grabbed Johnnie's arm.

"Come on."

We took a taxi at the corner. It was a short ride, and our feet hit the sidewalk almost before the cab had stopped. Martha Wain lived in one of those converted old townhouses near Central Park West in the Nineties. There was no answer to her buzzer, so I rang them all. We leaped up the stairs to the door with her name on a card. No sound answered our rap. For a second John Olds and I stared into each other's faces, then together leaned heavily in on the door. It gave, catapulting us into Martha Wain's living room. I heard a low exclamation from Johnnie. I stood horror-struck before the sight in the room.

The phone had been ripped out at the wall. Martha Wain sat with her back to us, leaning forward on a small secretary which must have held the phone. I heard John go into the hall—heard him vomit. I felt my stomach falling emptily, the blood drain from my lips. I forced myself to take a step forward, to look.

What had been the head of Martha Wain had been beaten into a greasy scarlet pulp. The blood dropped heavily from the shelf of the desk onto the green carpet. Shattered bits of bone; pulpy, beaten morsels of flesh and brain smattered the letter-paper, the body's blue dress. There was a black welt marking what had been the place where the neck met the spine. I went to the hall.

"All right now?"

Johnnie nodded sickly. I took a deep breath and went back into that room. I went closer than before and looked, steeling myself. For anything so horrible, it had been done in a great hurry, and neatly. Martha Wain's arm was warm. Then I found it. Through my natural horror a quiver of grim exultation leaped out, stilling the revulsion.

In Martha Wain's left hand was a small lock of hair, short and blond!

CHAPTER EIGHT

I sent Johnnie home, and called the police at the precinct I knew to be Inspector Dan Cassidy's. Then I took a quick look through Martha Wain's apartment. The small living room where we had found her body showed me nothing. It was full of the chintzy attempts of a woman living alone to bring warmth into a saddened New York brownstone. At that she hadn't done too badly, and I guessed that as an actress Martha Wain must have been in rather steady demand.

The bedroom was unexpectedly interesting. By all appearances, Martha Wain had expected to take a trip. The door to her clothes closet stood open, and one dress, still on its hanger, lay over her double bed. Open on the bed was a packed overnight bag. I thought furiously. I wanted to learn all I could before Cassidy arrived. Quickly I opened the bureau drawers, hunting. Nowhere in the bedroom could I find what I felt I must have next.

I returned to the living room. The only drawers in the room were in the lower part of that secretary, over which the body of Martha Wain leaned. Grimly, I ascertained that the blood had stopped dripping, and knelt down carefully beside the chair and its grisly burden. Slowly I drew the top drawer toward me, clear out. It was lucky that the secretary was shallow. I got the drawer out without touching her.

Her pocketbook was right on top. I dumped it onto the floor at my feet: lipstick, mirror, hairpins, compact, keys, three handkerchiefs, two letters, a billfold, a small calendar. I picked up the letters and looked at them. One was a letter from an agent. The second one had been mailed at Grand Central Annex. A hasty, scrawling backhand wrote:

Baby, I'll come on Sat. or Sun. Be ready. Don't take too much stuff. Don't say anything.

·It was unsigned. I hastily stuck it into my pocket, and picked up the billfold. Through its glassine window I could see a railroad ticket —New York to Pittsburgh, Pa., a one-way coach ticket. I took it out to examine it; it was stiff and new. I felt at last I had something to work on, something positive to add to the mystery of my vanished friend. A growing conviction flooded my mind as I steadily replaced the drawer.

I called the office and shook the city desk into action with a report of the murder. I had just finished the call when I heard steps on the stairs. Dan Cassidy rolled into the room, followed by two white-tuniced men with a stretcher between them.

"What's up, Sandy?" The Inspector knelt beside the body of the actress. "This is a helluva thing. . ."

"She phoned me, Inspector. I had asked if I could come up to talk to her about Mike Rawn tonight. I took up the phone at home to talk to her, and that must have been when she was killed."

A small, thin man came into the room. Dan Cassidy introduced him to me as the new coronor, Dr. Sumstein.

In a few minutes the doctor nodded to the two men in white coats, and they began to remove the body. He cleared his throat and said in a thin, high voice, "Died of concussion; heavy blow at the base of the skull. Killer beat her skull in fiendish rage. First blow killed her. Weapon like a sashweight or a small heavy baseball bat. So long, Cassidy. Pleased to meet you, Blunt."

The Inspector heard my story in detail. I told everything except finding the letter and the railroad ticket. Then I left. I walked over toward Broadway through the gathering crowd in front of the murder house, and turned south on Columbus. The street was wide, but dark, and I had gone about half the block between 95th and 94th when I began to sense I was being followed. I walked on, trying to listen for footsteps, but I heard none. When I reached the corner of Columbus and 94th, I looked back. There was no one walking on the sidewalk behind me, but about ten yards behind me a big black car was coming silently along, its lights very dim. I crossed Columbus and walked briskly west on 94th until I reached Broadway, where I turned again. The car had disappeared. In the dark, one car looks much like another, but I thought I recognized a huge limousine—the car that had · trailed me to the Automat the day after Mike disappeared.

I heard voices on the landing before the door of our apartment, and when I let myself in, two men besides Johnnie rose to greet me. One was Sam Cushman, the other a tall young man with a handsome face and shiny black hair.

Sam Cushman shook my hand. "Mr. Blunt, I brought along a member of the cast of Mike's show," he explained. "Mr. William Bush, Mr. Sandy Blunt. I think Mr. Bush may have something to tell you."

I told them of the murder of Martha Wain, and for a second I thought Johnnie was going to be sick again. Evidently he had said nothing to them. Bush seemed shocked, but Mr. Cushman sat suddenly, staring at me.

"Martha! Dead? Murdered?"

I smiled grimly. "I've just come from her apartment. What's wrong, Mr. Cushman?" I eyed him sharply. He lifted his eyes to mine and I felt a curtain falling, shutting me out.

He controlled his voice, after a minute asking, "Could I have a drink, please?"

"Sure," Johnnie stood up, glad to be doing something.

He returned quickly with filled glasses, and I turned to William Bush. "What is it you think I should know, Mr. Bush?"

"Well, I shared an upstairs dressing room with Floyd Harvey. He had to be at the theater for every performance, naturally. I had a small part in the play. The opening night we were all invited to Michael Rawn's party, and Floyd said he had to meet someone, and would I close his make-up box. I said I would. And that's what I have to tell you, Mr. Blunt."

"Yes?"

"It's this. In order to look the part of Michael if Michael should get sick, Floyd had bought a dark red wig. It had to be specially made, and cost him over one hundred dollars. He was very careful of it. Floyd left the theater before I was through on stage, so I didn't see him at all after the last curtain. But when I put his make-up away, I couldn't find the wig! He kept it in a small box inside the make-up box, and the box was there—but the wig just wasn't around anywhere! I hunted all over the dressing room for it. But I know it wasn't there." He stopped, and I thanked him.

Then I turned to Sam Cushman. "Mr. Cushman, I wonder if you'd give me a key to the theater? I'd like to go through Mike's dressing room, just to see if anything he left there might help me."

He took out a key-ring and handed me a largish key. "This is a master key; it will unlock all the doors in the theater," he said. "I'd be glad for you to keep it for as long as you feel you need it. I've been reading your stories on the disappearance, and I'm glad to help." Sam Cushman rose and William Bush with him.

"If there is anything I can do, Mr. Blunt," Bush said, "just let me know. Mr. Cushman can reach me."

"Fine; thank you. Mr. Cushman, you've closed the show?"

He nodded sadly. "It was all I could do. If I could find anyone to handle Mike's part, the show would be a hit, with all the publicity it's getting. . ." he smiled wanly, "but it's impossible."

They said good-bye. Johnnie got ready for bed, and I sketched out a quick release and phoned it to Pat Curry. He was jubilant. The police were in an uproar, throwing a dragnet around the city, and the *Globe* had a terrific scoop on the Wain murder.

"Stick in that theater loop, Blunt," Curry rasped, "maybe all those red asbestos babies will kill one another . . ." With a hearty laugh at the prospect, he hung up.

Johnnie was snoring, and I went into the kitchen and made myself some coffee. I tried to figure out why Martha Wain had been killed. It would make a good newspaper yarn, right or wrong. And it might bring me to Michael, for obviously she had been killed because she had found out what had happened to Michael Rawn. I felt certain the only connection she had with Mike had been through her husband. I was the last person who had seen him alive. Still there was no motive, so far as Mike's disappearance was concerned. No ransom notes, nothing. Yet the same night Mike had gone, his understudy, Floyd Harvey, had also disappeared. Martha had been friendly with Mike. For more reasons than one Floyd might have been deadly jealous of Michael Rawn. I took the scrawled note out of my pocket, the one that had been posted at Grand Central Annex. The writing was not Mike's fine, determined hand; of that I was certain. I would use that note in my next story. I stuffed it back into my pocket, thinking of that big car that had followed me away from Wain's.

I was not getting anywhere, merely torturing myself. To think of Mike being held somewhere, starved, perhaps, more likely at the mercy of a jealousy-maddened killer—that was tough enough without sitting down and not trying to do anything about it. I took out the large master key that Cushman had given me. I listened and could hear Johnnie's even snoring. Slowly and noiselessly I tiptoed into the studio room, and from my bureau got my small flashlight. The clock said one o'clock when I left the house.

I took the subway to Times Square and walked north a few blocks through the thinning revellers, then turned west and walked toward the theater where Johnnie and I had seen Mike's one-night triumph. There was hardly anyone on the block as I turned down the alley to the dark stage door. Quietly I let myself in with my key.

It was pitch black inside, an amphitheater of emptiness. I could feel rather than see the wide, high spaces of darkness that filled every corner. I fumbled my way to a steel ladder near the proscenium arch, and climbed to what looked, in the dim light of my suppressed flashlight, to be the light-bridge. There was a chalk-written word beside a switch bigger than the rest. *Work-lite,* it said, and I turned it on. A grim spot of light appeared on the stage, another backstage, behind the set where Mike's public self had come to life. I clambered down and hunted for the dressing rooms.

The name Michael Rawn still marked the large dressing room on the same floor as the stage, and I opened the door and went in. The room had been newly furnished for Mike, I judged, for the carpentry looked new and the paint was unmarked with the usual daubs of grease-paint and fingermarks. I opened Mike's clothes closet, and got a jolt. Inside it were the three suits I recognized as the ones Mike had worn in the play. And beside them, still on its hanger, unworn and untouched, was a full set of formal tails! I flashed my light onto the floor. Mike came close to me in the neat row of shoes, three for the play, and the patent leather ones for dress.

Dress! For his own party, of course! Mike had never dressed for his party at all! He had left in a great hurry; had not had time to change his clothes! Then I stopped my thoughts. I was wrong. Mike *had* changed. He *must* have. The three acts of the play, as to costume, were here. And the logical change from the last act of the play would be into his dress clothes for his party. No. Mike had changed, all right, but he had left the theater in the same clothes he had worn when he came into the theater—the same clothes he had worn when he called on Johnnie and me! In a flash I recalled the handsome light brown tweed suit with matching topcoat. Wherever Mike Rawn had gone, he had worn those clothes.

Outside Mike's dressing room door I found a metal box, the size of a big lunch-box. In the light of my flash I examined it. It was Mike's make-up box. I took out the shelf with its tubes of paint, its rabbit foot for rouge, and looked into the bottom. My heart leaped. Rolled up on the bottom was a dark reddish wig!

I flashed my light up on the walls. I could see rising in tiers above me the doors of the other dressing rooms, leading onto several iron balconies. At the end was a landing onto a circular iron stairway leading onto the floor of the backstage. I started up, after closing Mike's make-up box carefully and putting it at the foot of the stairway. I wanted to see the dressing room of Floyd Harvey, where by all reason I ought to have found that wig. I hardly knew what I was looking for, but anything, I felt, would help me now. I went to the top of the rickety stair, and walked along the iron balcony, flashing my light on the doors as I went. I stopped before a door that had Bush-Harvey written on it.

It was a big room, built to house the chorus of a musical. There were about ten mirrors on each side of the room, with a shelf below them. Two of the many chairs in the room had been thrust close to the shelf, and on them were two make-up boxes. I moved toward the chairs—and found myself listening intently. I could have sworn I heard a creak, like a footstep on an old board. Slowly, carefully, my heart beating in my ears, I retraced my steps to the dressing room door, high above the level of the floor. It came again. The step seemed far from me, across the space, on the other side of the stage— perhaps in the dress circle of the theater. The work lights still marked a pale white circle on the stage set, and on the backstage area. I looked down into the set as into a house with the roof cut away. Nothing moved. I listened for a long time, then put it down to tightened nerves, and returned to my searching.

I found nothing, and felt it useless to go through the other rooms. Returning to the stage, I found I was sleepy and tired, and I decided to go home. I reached down at the foot of the iron stair to pick up Mike's make-up box. It had disappeared!

My heart began to thump again. I had been right. There *was* someone else in the building! I started to investigate; a surge of pure rage rolled over me at being watched night and day, followed, anticipated. I stepped through a property door onto the stage set, more angry than anything else. Muslin covers had been thrown over the elegant chairs on the set . . . . suddenly my muscles tensed and I leaped like a jack-rabbit to one side. There was a faint swoosh—I whirled just in time to see a huge sandbag clump tremendously into the chair I had just passed, breaking the legs off at the seat, splaying them out like the legs of a spider! I watched transfixed as the bag slowly leaned over and fell onto the stage heavily. My staring eyes saw the black stenciled letters—SAND—100 POUNDS.

Suddenly I quivered with fury. I leaped across the stage to the side opposite the dressing rooms. There was a thin steel ladder. I flashed my light up; it diluted into greyness. I surged up the ladder, and as I went I could hear footsteps, clear now, racing above me. I knew that I was chasing the killer, Mike's abductor; hate and fear gave me strength and speed. I got to the top of the ladder and found myself on a grid-work, high above the tiny white spots of light on the stage below me. I kept my light low, to see where I was putting my feet. I was close to the roof of the theater; the grid seemed to be a flooring that completely covered the roof of the theater behind the audience opening. There was a scrambling; I moved toward it. As I did, I heard footsteps again, clear and running, above me. There was a way to get to the roof, and the killer was escaping.

Then I saw the opening. It was a trap door, and showed itself as a light square in the ink-dark roof. I could no longer hear the footsteps as I hoisted myself through the opening, after a minute's fumbling finding a box the murderer must have used before me.

I reached the edge of the roof and looked down into an alley behind the theater. There was a fire escape. As I watched, a dark figure ran to the intersection, into the lights of the street, turned the corner and was lost in the milling mob of pleasure seekers.

I sat down on the top step of the fire escape, and swore richly. I had found and lost a clue, been nearly killed, and seen the killer of Martha Wain, the abductor of my friend. And I had nothing to show for all of it but the experience.

CHAPTER NINE

The next day was Monday, the first of November, and I woke at 10 and dressed to take my story into the office. Pat Curry hailed me.

"Blunt, your stuff is all right. Keep it up!"

I smiled sourly, telling him of my experience of the night before. He nodded. "Good! Great going; keep in the middle of it! I've kept in touch with Cassidy; he hasn't got as much as you have. If he comes onto anything I'll get it to you right away. Just keep it up, boy!"

I was thanking him when the door opened and Lisa Cushman came in.

"Hello, Sandy!" she greeted me and turned to Pat Curry. "I had hoped to find you if you're Mr. Curry," she went on. Curry looked at me and then at Lisa.

"You're Miss Cushman? Sit down."

"I'll stand, thank you. Mr. Curry, I've come to tell you that I would be very much pleased if you would stop referring to me in your news columns as the *Sweetheart of the Missing*."

Pat Curry nodded judiciously. "All right, Miss Cushman. Your father has always given us co-operation; I think it can be arranged to your satisfaction."

Lisa Cushman rose and held out her hand. "Thank you very much, Mr. Curry."

I spoke up. "If you aren't busy, I'd like to take you to lunch, Lisa."

"I'd love it, thank you, Sandy."

I took her arm and we left. I didn't say that I had coined the phrase *Sweetheart of the Missing*—there was no use making life more complicated than it was already.

We went to Stouffers on 42nd and Park Avenue, and when I had ordered, Lisa asked, "Have you found out anything definite about Mike, Sandy?"

I looked at her directly. "Why did you take the old letters from Mike's safe, Lisa?"

Her face became guarded at once. "What letters, Sandy?"

I thought of that falling sandbag and my lips tightened. "Don't waltz me around, Lisa; last night someone tried to kill me." I told her about the missing make-up box with the wig, about the near escape, the fleeing dark form. Her face became serious.

"Sandy," she said, "I may as well tell you—I did take those letters. You'll just have to trust me about them. They were mine, they belonged to me. More I can't tell you. But I just had to have them. That's all. Please don't ask me to tell you any more."

I felt sick. Here I was batting my brains out finding the guy she was in love with; and I knew too damn well what was happening to me, but she couldn't trust me with her confidence.

"It's all right, Lisa, if that's how you want it," I replied.

"It's how it's got to be," Lisa said softly.

Our meal wasn't much of a success. We talked of Mike and of his plans, and what could have happened to him. Once she said: "Mike was entirely different than anyone knew; he had great things in him."

"I knew Mike well; he was a great man," I stated flatly.

"I often wondered what had happened to make him so . . . . . alone;

so completely beyond the world, you might say," she mused.

Briefly, I told Lisa about what Johnnie and I had found in the papers; concluding with my guess that something or someone had cropped up out of that terrible past to haunt Mike, perhaps to cause him to run away, more likely to kidnap him out of revenge.

As I told my story, a peculiar thing happened. When I finished, I looked Lisa full in the face. She looked stiffly before her, as though she had seen a ghost. I thought she was going to faint.

"What's wrong, Lisa? Can I do something?"

"No; no, . . .I'm all right, Sandy. . . .it's just. . . ." She rose and put one hand on my arm. "I've got to go, Sandy, right now. I can't stay any longer. . . .we'll see each other again. . . .thanks, and good-bye for now. . . ." She left so quickly I was staring after her, standing there by our table, when the dessert came. I had no heart for it; I paid and left.

. I went home and rambled the empty apartment, trying to think myself out of my dilemma. I had no way of tracing the letters now. Lisa had said they were hers. Biglow said they were far too old for that. Had Mike told Lisa to take care of them if anything happened? More and more I began to feel that Mike had expected something to happen to him; that gallant as he was he would never own that such a feeling should enter into his plans for the future. In small ways he had tried to protect himself. But where he had gone, how he had been spirited away, why anyone would want to risk discovery by stealing that red wig under my nose—all of it escaped me as much as the murder of Martha Wain defied detection. However, I had thought over the affair of Martha Wain, and had come to a conclusion which seemed to hold water.

She must have known something about the disappearance of Mike, to begin with. Perhaps she was some sort of accessory. But her confederate, who was doing the real work, got worried about her. She must be silenced. Somehow the confederate discovered that she was trying to leave town, to get away from what she had begun to fear. He wrote her the note I had taken, to make certain she would be at home, and had come just in time to hear her give way to her fright by phoning to me, to tell what she knew. And standing behind her as she lifted the phone, the killer had bludgeoned her to death.

I tried to think of one loose end I had not tried, and a sudden thought took hold of me. Mike was always firm about having money in the bank. And there was every evidence that he had quite a lot of money. I phoned Biglow and found that Michael had been a steady customer at the Trent Bank of America, 50th Street Branch. With a feeling of discovery I hustled into my coat and jumped into a cab.

As I rode across town I pulled from my pocket a typewritten sheet I had made of everything I had learned to date. It seemed pitifully inadequate, but it was the best I could do. I considered carefully. I had talked with everyone who had known Michael any length of time; they were few enough. Jasmine Le Valley, Sam Cushman, Lisa, Martha Wain . . . . everyone I had been able to interview had given me all they knew. But the information had no pattern, the bits of fact had no mortar to hold them into any integrated structure. I hadn't the time to go into all the years of Mike's past; the only connection had been Lady Matilda Wintarthur, and she was exhausted as a source of information. All in all, it was a discouraging sheet of paper, no antidote for the aura of horror and mystery I felt stealthily closing around me.

An official at the bank introduced me immediately to a Mr. Bleeker when I announced my business. Mr. Bleeker was a hesitant, pedantic man in blue serge, who toyed continually with a fountain pen. He seemed worried. He was, he said, a paying teller.

"I'm glad to have this opportunity to speak to you, Mr. Blunt," he eased himself; "because while I don't want to violate the confidence of one of our depositors, I still feel that . . . . well, I've been reading your articles, and perhaps there is something of interest here . . . ."

"What is it you want to tell me, Mr. Bleeker? I assure you your name or connection need not be mentioned."

"Thank you, Mr. Blunt. Well, what I have to tell is, you might say . . . ." he laughed feebly, "somewhat of a series itself. You see, I had handled Mr. Rawn's deposits, and my wife and I had bought tickets for Mr. Rawn's play the opening night. It was an expense, but it was our anniversary, and she said to me . . . ."

"But you were telling me about Mr. Rawn's deposits. . . ."

"Oh, yes. Well, I had handled all of Mr. Rawn's business here— I rather felt there was a personal bond between us. . ."

"Was there anything particular, Mr. Bleeker; anything out of the ordinary at all? That's what I would be interested in."

He pulled up short, and thought deeply, finally announcing, "Yes. I hope you will regard this as confidential." I nodded, and he went on. "Mr. Rawn has, for some time, been carefully and quite regularly withdrawing his savings. Naturally, that was his business. But the sums have been quite large, and he disregarded my suggestion to see our investment counsel. Mr. Rawn withdrew large sums, yet always in bills of small denomination. But the last withdrawal was just this morning; and I was about to get in touch with someone in authority —except that the transaction was legal and I had no actual reason for complaint. Put yourself in my position, Mr. Blunt. I dare not offend, yet must bear the responsibility were anything to go wrong. . . ."

"What happened this morning?"

"The last check on Mr. Rawn's account was honored," Mr. Bleeker said, uncomfortably, "and Mr. Rawn's book was presented, closing Mr. Rawn's account. It was a check for one thousand dollars! It was properly endorsed, the signature compared in every respect with Mr. Rawn's, and I turned over the money, closing Mr. Rawn's account with us."

"What made that extraordinary?"

Mr. Bleeker twirled the pen. "Nothing, Mr. Blunt—except that it *was not Mr. Rawn who closed the account.* And it is an exception for the very last transaction to be done by anyone else; it is the one bank transaction that usually the depositor himself tends to."

"Who took the money?" I inquired eagerly. "What did he look like?"

"I was careful to remember him," Mr. Bleeker allowed; "because in many ways he resembled Mr. Rawn. The man who closed Mr. Rawn's account had blue eyes, and his hair was light, and close-cropped."

I felt my breath quicken. "How much money had Mr. Rawn on deposit when he first began to withdraw?"

Mr. Bleeker hesitated one second, then said in a quiet voice: "Mr. Rawn was wealthy; his account with us reached its peak at two hundred thousand dollars."

My head swam; I *knew* Mike could never have saved that kind of money. After all, as Johnnie put it, it was only three years! I did not speak; for with the shock of finding Michael Rawn a rich man I had come upon the man I was looking for—the man who had tried to kill me, had escaped, and had coolly gone into Mike's bank the next morning and taken the last of Mike's money. And had been black-mailing Mike for some time before, I guessed. When Mike refused payment any longer, he had kidnapped Mike for his own safety.

I thanked Mr. Bleeker, assured him of my discretion, and returned thoughtfully to the apartment. Once there I had an inspiration. I sat down at the phone, dialing Cushman's office. It took just a few moments to get the chirping Miss McGonigle to give me the last address she had in her files for Floyd Harvey.

Floyd Harvey's room was small, with a window on the street. The bed had been slept in, but when I could not tell. I turned on the light and looked around. There were theater programs, with the name Floyd Harvey underlined; a book of plays, some ticket stubs stuck in the mirror edges. I opened the clothes closet, and took the clothes and dumped them, hangers and all, onto the bed. I made a discovery.

Along with the clothes that I guessed had belonged to Floyd Harvey, of ordinary make and built for a heavy man, were garments I recognized. There were a pair of pigskin gloves, a brown tweed suitcoat, and a tie that I myself had given to Mike. I returned to the closet. On the floor I found a pair of shoes. I recognized them at once. They were the perfect, small shoes that Michael had worn when he called at our apartment the night of his disappearance.

One thing was very clear. Mike had been brought to this room. He had been here since his disappearance. It was natural that he would be moved, taken away. If Floyd Harvey had meant to keep him away, perhaps later kill him after he forced Mike to turn over that money to him, Floyd Harvey would know it would not be long until someone would come hunting that room.

I threw the clothes over my arm, and took the shoes in my hand. I meant to examine them thoroughly back at the apartment, and then to turn them over to Cassidy. But I wanted to go over every wrinkle and seam of the clothes that belonged to Michael Rawn.

The housekeeper who had let me in came past the door, and I called, "I beg your pardon, but do you know whether this room has been occupied since Mr. Harvey's disappearance?"

"No, I don't know that. Mr. Harvey did not like me to clean it. He did all his own work—there wasn't much of it, he said. I ain't been in there for almost two weeks. I used to go in maybe once a month to scrub, but that's all."

"Thank you very much." She drifted away upstairs, adjuring me to close the door when I was through.

I took one last look around, moving about the room to make sure I had missed nothing. I felt certain I had seen everything that had been left in the room; felt I had been right to come here when I did. As I left, my foot caught on the carpet where it lifted over the leg of the one arm-chair in the room. I stooped to straighten it, and what I saw made me throw my armful of clothing onto the bed. I stooped feverishly, tearing the carpet back, rolling it up off the old parquet wooden floor, and stood for a long time staring at that floor.

Hidden by the carpet was a sizeable stain of dark brown, irregular and dried.

CHAPTER TEN

The next day I received the strange phone call. I had gone to the office, filed a story with Pat Curry, and dodged over to the precinct station to see if I could find Inspector Dan Cassidy. As he was out of his office, I took myself back to the Globe Building. I felt the need to talk to someone about Michael Rawn, and I thought I would wait for Johnnie to finish, since it was late afternoon.

Pat Curry was pleased with the handling I was giving the "Mike Rawn thing," as he called it, and told me so.

"I expect you to make the grade, Blunt," he admitted grudgingly. I just nodded, too beaten to care very much. He went on encouragingly, "Don't let it get you down. A lot worse things could happen. Hell, even if they never find this Rawn, you got a set-up!"

"I want to find Mike." In my mind I was seeing again that splotch of brown stain beneath the carpet on 88th Street. I had told Dan Cassidy about it, and he informed me that Dr. Sumstein's chemist had said it was human blood.

"I know, Blunt, but these things happen to every reporter." Curry warmed to his subject, and I knew I was in for the history of his cub days in Chicago. The phone rang, and Curry picked it up, listened, and handed it to me.

"Yes?" I asked listlessly.

What I heard sounded like a woman's voice, but I couldn't be certain. There was a great effort at disguising it.

"Mr. Blunt? New York Globe?"

"This is he. Who is this?"

"That don't matter," the voice said. "I'm just warning you to get those letters. The letters in the pink ribbon. I'm warning you, that's all. You understand me?"

"Are they your letters?" I asked.

"Yes, they're mine. And I want them. Hear me?"

I tried to prolong the conversation, but the voice hung up. I got the operator, but she said the call was from a pay station and couldn't be traced. Pat Curry was curious.

"Something new?"

"No. Just someone wanting his name in print, that's all." I felt like a dog lying to him, and didn't do it very well. But I remembered Lisa and the batch of letters, the same letters she had said were hers. I stalked once or twice over to the windows and looked down at the East River, then dialed the Cushman number.

"This is the Cushman's," a male voice said quietly.

"Miss Cushman, please."

"One moment, sir." There was a pause, then her voice poured into my ear.

"Lisa, this is Sandy. If you have more time than the last meal we had together, I'd like to take you to dinner."

"I can't tonight, Sandy. I'm promised to a Charity Ball. But if the offer holds for tomorrow, I'd love it."

"The offer holds forever," I suddenly blurted. There was a short pause, then she laughed. I said I'd call for her. Pat Curry was watching me as I turned from the phone.

"I don't know what the hell to do," I confessed. "I think I know who killed Martha Wain; I'm certain I do. I have the feeling that the mystery of Mike and the murder of Martha Wain are just two parts of the same crime. But I can't prove it."

Pat Curry gave me his mirthless grin. "What's the matter; getting scared? Hell, you're just getting into this! Cassidy doesn't know a goddam thing more than you do. I promised him a page spread with his ugly mug at the top if he'd give me something special. He admitted he had nothing! For Chrissake, don't show yellow now."

"Listen," I argued, "I've got a special reason for wanting to find . . ."

He broke in, his eyes shrewd. "Sure you do! You're falling like a load of flatfooted bricks for Cushman—it's written all over your big pan! But keep after Harvey—he's the killer; Jeez, Blunt!" .

"All right!" I yelled back, "So I'm falling for her! What good does it do me?"

Pat Curry eyed me for a minute, then his voice lowered.

"Not a damn bit of good if you find Rawn." He indicated a chair. "Sit down, Blunt, and get it out of your system. Now what's the dope, as of right now? Come on, give out."

I met his eye and he ticked his head as I listed, "All right, listen to this. A pair of scissors missing, Mike's suitcoat, gloves, shoes, tie on 88th Street, blood on the floor and no tenant. The brushes that left Mike's old apartment but didn't get to the Park Avenue place. A batch of letters stolen—Lisa Cushman says they're hers, Biglow the valet says they can't be, and two other parties claim them. All unrelated, and every bit of it part of the picture! Not to mention a guy who calls me, then is out of town when I call—and to top it off someone who tries to kill me so he can steal a damn red wig!"

Pat Curry rubbed his hands together, his eyes glinting. "Jeez, Blunt! What a chance!" He glared at me, thrusting his face into mine. "Listen, you Swedish dodo, I'm going to make a writer of you yet! You get on this thing and I don't give a damn if everyone in New York takes a shot at you, you stay on it until you get the killer! Get me?"

I stood up. "Hell, what have I been doing? I don't want to be anywhere else! I'd just like something in this screwy case to break, that's all!"

"If it doesn't break; *make* it! Go out and shoot someone yourself if it gets on your nerves! But keep going! This is the biggest thing in years! Find me another body like that Wain woman and I'll give you a raise! Now get going." I started for the door and his voice cracked like a whip; "Blunt!"

I turned, my mouth a straight line. Goddam Simon Legree, the White Slaver.

"What is it?"

"Who is that monkey you room with; the one in the art department?"

"John Olds."

Suddenly he leaned toward me, his fists on the desk before him. "For God's sake, Blunt; don't you ever feel the need of a drink?"

"Hell, yes."

"Well," he thrust, "get the stinking hell out of here and get one. I need one from just looking at you! And pick up Olds to go with you. You need a keeper. If you get a story tomorrow, send him in with it. I don't want to see you around! On your way!"

I left without a word, my insides threshing with anger. In the lobby I met Johnnie.

"What's the dope?" he demanded. "I'm minding my own business when along comes the boss and says Curry tells him I'm to get out for the rest of the day! What the hell?"

I looked at him disgustedly. "That blue-bellied Curry; has to

67

slit your throat and step on your face before he does something for you . . ."

"What do you mean?"

"Listen," I informed him, "you're looking at a very confused man. My soul is torn; you're to come and hold my head tonight. We're eating on the company, and getting to bed early. The hell with Curry. You don't have to come in tomorrow if you don't want to." Johnnie's presence made me feel better. He was the one person I could safely talk to.

"Listen, will I?" Johnnie mocked. "I don't have to be told when I'm in luck. Tell you what let's do—if you're not feeling like a big time. We'll go home, wash up, have a quiet dinner at the C. & L., and talk everything out and go to bed. Seems I haven't seen you, Sandy, since you started to hunt for Mike."

It was good to hear him tell me what I needed more than anything in the world. I was tired, and excited over being potted at; I could still hear that ugly whisper of sound as the sand-bag dropped like death itself into the chair. Worst of all, I could recall all too easily that stencil on the canvas cover—SAND, 100 POUNDS.

We had a long dinner at the C. & L., and talked out everything I had learned. Johnnie admitted that he couldn't piece it together any better than I had.

"It doesn't seem like one crime at all, Mike's disappearance," I cogitated. "It's more like several parts of two crimes or more."

"How do you mean?" Johnnie Olds questioned.

"Well," I frowned, "I figure this way: Mike's disappearance is connected with the murder of Martha Wain through her husband, the understudy." A thought caused me to snap my fingers. "Listen to this theory. Floyd Harvey is separated from his wife, but still loves her. She is trying to better herself, and makes for Mike. Floyd has the part as the understudy in the show; feels he is Mike's understudy in private life. He manages to kidnap Mike and holds him somewhere. But Martha Wain has heard Floyd threaten to do something of the sort, and she doesn't want to be a part of it. She threatens in her turn to give Floyd away. He knows he has gone too far, but can't go back. He kills her just as she tries to tell me what she knows . . ."

"It's all right if it will hold together."

"If that were all, it would be easy. We *know* everything we need. Motive, opportunity—all of it is there." I spread my hands gloomily. "But how about the other items? They can't be shrugged off!"

"For instance?"

I repeated for Johnnie the miscellaneous items, mysterious yet compelling, that I had spoken of to Pat Curry earlier in the day. Johnnie nodded his head slowly as I finished.

"You know a lot, Sandy," he admitted very quietly, "and you're right; they don't fit into the theory you have. Unless it's that business of Mike's money."

I nodded, and added, "That could be part of Floyd's scheme, at that. He might have been holding Mike until he got all the money—and now that he has it . . ." Our eyes met and held for an electric moment.

"You'll find Mike all right," Johnnie said slowly.

My voice was stiff when I answered. Our conversation had brought me up short before an appalling fact. "Floyd has Mike's money; he has no reason now for keeping Mike alive."

Johnnie made no answer. We both knew it was true. It could be no other way. If Floyd Harvey had been holding Mike somewhere, every day Mike went on living, knowing what Floyd had done, made Mike that much bigger risk for the killer of Martha Wain. Harvey had murdered once, brutally and with terrible deliberation. Mike had from the first been his object of revenge. Harvey would not hesitate to kill a second time.

We sat silent a minute. I cursed myself for an abject idiot. I could so easily have guessed that Mike had money in a bank somewhere—we had all talked about it often enough in the old days. Mike had always preferred checking accounts; and had said so. And everywhere I had gone in the past few days I had had clear signs of Mike's prosperity. A moment's forethought would have told me to hunt up a bank; tell them to hold anyone who tried to pick up Mike's money in cash. I would probably have saved Mike's life, and caught the killer of Martha Wain. Johnnie leaned toward me.

"Don't blame yourself, Sandy," he chided. "You did the best you could. Cassidy knows all this. The police are busy. You did everything you could. But where did Mike get all that money?"

I shrugged with exasperation. "That's easy enough. You and I both knew that. Remember in those old papers reading about the unnamed socialite who had established a trust fund for Michael to go to college? Well, that's where the money came from. The unnamed socialite is Lady Matilda Wintarthur, of course. She put money in

69

trust for Mike, and felt she had done her share. That's why she felt she didn't ever need to see him. He must have received the capital when he was twenty-one."

"I never thought of that . . ."

Our talk petered out into thoughts. At last Johnnie said, "We don't want to sit here thinking ourselves into a dark hole, Sandy."

We rose and went back to the apartment. Johnnie poured us a stiff drink. As he gave me mine, he frowned.

"The thing that makes it so tough about Mike's disappearing, as I see it, is that we are the only people who knew him well at all."

As he spoke, a sudden idea jolted me. It was new, and might be important. I phoned Pat Curry and asked him if he could locate the name and address of Jasmine Le Valley's mother. He said he would call me back. When I hung up, Johnny was staring at me.

"What's the idea?"

I smiled grimly. "I've just thought of the one person who might really know Michael Rawn; the only person beside the two of us."

I had hardly finished speaking when the phone rang. It was Curry. "The dope you needed was in the files. Got a pencil?" He gave me the address of Mrs. Jessie Martin, 19 Flery Way, Flatbush, and told me how to get there. I hung up and shrugged into my topcoat.

"Where are you going now?" Johnnie demanded. "I thought you wanted to get some sleep tonight?"

"Some other time will do. I got a trip to make. A little social call, my friend."

It took me nearly an hour to find 19 Flery Way, Flatbush. It was a small house, all on one floor, practically in the country. I could see a big yard stretching out behind the house as I went up the walk and rang the bell.

A woman opened the door on a chain, and peeped out.

"Who is it?"

"Mr. Blunt, a friend of your daughter."

She opened the door and asked me in. I entered a small living room, furnished in overstuffed mohair, replete with antimacassars and bric-a-brac. She turned on a pink-silk shaded lamp. I began right away.

"The *Globe* has put me on the disappearance of Michael Rawn; I'm a reporter, Mrs. Martin. Your daughter told me you had known Michael for some time before his disappearance. Is there anything you could tell me? Was he worried about anything that he spoke to you about?"

. She bit her lip and put a hand to her straight hair, done high in a bun on her head. She could have been a suburban housewife anywhere. I would never have guessed her to be the mother of flashy Jasmine Le Valley.

"No sir, he didn't mention anything to me." A touch of pride crept into her voice. "Mr. Rawn was going to do a book about my daughter's life and her career. He was a very friendly young man; made me nice company, I must say."

"What did you talk about, Mrs. Martin?"

"Well, let me see. My daughter, mostly. He helped me around the place like he was . . . well, just like one of the family, you might say."

I pressed her. I had expected to learn more. "Just how did Michael help you, Mrs. Martin?"

She made a meaningless gesture. "Well, just around the house. He told me to go right on with whatever I was doing whenever he would come in the front door . . . so I would just go ahead. And he would pick up a dust-cloth and help me. That's all . . ."

"Did you tell him about your daughter's career, Mrs. Martin?"

"Oh, no—he knew about that. He just wanted background, Mr. Blunt. He fed the chickens, and burned papers, and helped me in the kitchen. He was a very nice young man," she repeated, smiling timidly.

She seemed to veer away from something that was worrying her, so I took the leap. "Mrs. Martin, I'd like to help you. What's on your mind? I'll keep it strictly off the record if you wish."

She sighed, thought a long minute. I spoke again. "Did anything happen in the months you knew Michael Rawn?"

Suddenly it burst out of her, like dammed water. "Mr. Blunt, I've been so worried! I couldn't think it . . . but my daughter . . . Myrtle is her real name . . . well, she says something is gone from her bureau . . . well, she is *sure* something is missing . . . but I *never* touch her private things, Mr. Blunt . . ."

"What is it that your daughter is missing?"

"I don't know if it means anything; if it can help you . . ."

"When did your daughter miss it?"

"Oh, just lately, Mr. Blunt . . . but neither of us know just when it disappeared . . . I don't even know . . ."

71

"What is missing, Mrs. Martin?" I asked desperately.

"Some letters," she said, wringing her hands, "some old letters in a pink ribbon."

I tried not to show my excitement. "When did your daughter miss them?"

"Well," she computed, "maybe a week ago . . . not any longer than that . . . but I don't know . . ."

"Don't know what, Mrs. Martin . . . ?"

"Well, Mr. Blunt, I hate to say it, it may mean nothing . . . but Myrtle thinks that maybe Mr. Rawn took the letters . . . for the book. He had been working on notes for it almost six months."

"And you'd like me to get them back for her; is that it?"

Her eyes implored me. "Oh, Mr. Blunt, if only you would. I never knew Myrtle to take on so about anything. Maybe you could put an ad in the paper . . ."

I smiled. "Maybe I can do better than that, Mrs. Martin. I can't promise." I rose. "Your daughter isn't certain when—just what time they disappeared."

"No, Mr. Blunt," her eyes widened, "and I don't know either. If . . . I don't think so myself, but . . . if Mr. Rawn took them . . . they might have been gone for a long time."

It was half-past eleven when I reached the apartment. John was still up: "Well; do any good?"

"She said Mike was a *very* nice man, and she said it often," I told John, ". . . *and* that he stole some letters belonging to her daughter, Jasmine Le Valley, the burlesque queen, of all people!"

"The letters in the pink ribbon? My God, how many people does that make, wanting those letters?"

"Four that I know of . . ."

"They must be important, at that. Whose do *you* think they really are?"

I eyed him meditatively. "I think they are very old," I replied slowly, "and I think they really belong to Michael Rawn."

CHAPTER ELEVEN

I stood in the foyer of Lisa Cushman's apartment building tapping my hat against my knee. She kept me waiting just three minutes by my watch, when the elevator doors opened and she came toward me.

I felt a lump rise in my throat. Lisa was a very beautiful woman.
"Hello, Sandy . . ."

I mumbled a greeting, and took her arm. The cab started down Fifth Avenue, both of us in our corners. I hate a guy who can't get into a taxi with a woman without reaching for her. If she wants you, you know it.

"Where are we going?" Lisa asked.

"A little place in the Village. I'd like to have a long talk."

She laughed. "My, Sandy, you sound grim."

"I feel grim." I told her about my latest discoveries, and felt her stiffen at the tale of the dark stain under the carpet in the room where I had found Michael's belongings.

"Did you go over Michael's clothing? Did you find anything?"

I nodded despondently. "No. They look all right to me. I'm positive there aren't any stains on Mike's clothes. I turned them over to Dan Cassidy this morning. He squawked, but I think he was glad to get any sort of lead."

A pause lengthened, then Lisa spoke, with an urgency that startled me for an instant. "Sandy," she declared in a low voice, "you've *got* to find him! You've got to find Michael Rawn—soon!"

She leaned over to me, and I faced her in the cab. I felt her hand reach for mine, and I closed my hand over hers. It was cold.

"I'll find him. And it will be soon," I declared, feeling like a deceiving fool as I said it. Mike's kidnaping was enigmatic, and now it seemed to grow over me like some great swarming cloud, threatening to shut out all light from my mind; threatening to shut out my life itself.

Her voice sunk to a whisper. "You don't realize how important it is, Sandy; how desperate Mike's disappearance is making me . . ."

I turned again to look at her, and my hand fell to my side. Once again it swept over me, the sickness that shook me to my deepest heart. I was hunting Mike, I knew it was mine to do. I was certainly the only one who with reason might be expected to find Michael Rawn. And God help me, I had fallen so deeply in love with Mike's girl that it made me sick to hear her wish him back. I could feel the muscles working at the sides of my jaw.

"I'll find him; don't let it worry you, Lisa . . ."

Her tone changed, and she said swiftly, "But . . . Sandy . . . you don't know . . ."

I interrupted impatiently. "I don't need to be told everything,

73

Lisa," I informed her stolidly.

There was another long silence, and during it the cab dropped us on West 8th Street, before the *Jumble Shop*. The silence hung between us like a blanket held by the corners, wet and dripping, as we sought a table.

When our cocktails came, Lisa leaned across the table and put her hand over mine. I tightened my lips and started to move my hand, but she broke in nurriedly.

"Don't, Sandy. I want us to be friends, please."

I looked into her eyes. I knew she was in earnest, and God knows I wanted to be friends.

"I'm sorry, Lisa," I apologized. "I'm acting like a kid, when the last thing in the world I want to do is anything that will give you more worry than you have now. Forgive me. I'll get straightened around; this business of Mike's vanishing has got me going in circles, that's all."

"I know, Sandy, and it's the hardest thing anyone ever had to do; hunt for his friend. Everything will come out all right; I know it will. You'll find him all right."

I looked directly into her deep eyes. "Do you think Mike is dead? Tell me the truth, Lisa."

Her answer surprised me. She returned my steady look, and her answer was quick enough, but it seemed well-prepared and long considered—not an answer given simply to allay my feelings.

"No, Sandy. I do not believe Mike is dead. I don't think . . . he's dead—yet . . ." Then that strange tone of urgency returned to her voice. "But you've got to hurry, Sandy."

"Lisa, tell me," I suddenly heard myself say, "you know more than you're letting me know, aren't you? What do you know about Mike's disappearance, Lisa? Tell me."

She looked away from me for a moment when the first course came, then she went on, very quietly. "I don't know anything, not really Sandy, or I'd tell you. You know I would. All I know . . . is guessing."

My smile was thin. "And what do you guess?"

She spoke carefully and slowly, as though putting her thoughts in measured order. "Well, when father told me he was going to have to close the show because he couldn't replace Michael, I began to think just who could profit by Mike's . . . being taken away. The only person I could think of was Floyd Harvey, but he had gone, and then

74

his wife, Martha Wain, was murdered. But Harvey and Martha had been separated, even though they occasionally went places together. I remember they arrived together that night at Michael's party, so I tried to recall anyone who knew Floyd Harvey . . ."

"Good," I commented, "and then?"

"I had been to some of the rehearsals, and I remembered that Floyd had sat in the audience most of the time when Michael himself was rehearsing, and he had talked quite a lot to a girl who had a small part in Mike's play. Joyce Bennet, her name was. Do you remember her? Have you questioned any members of the cast, Sandy?"

I shook my head. "I've meant to go over them all, but I haven't had the time, along with the stories and everything else that have come up. Which one was Joyce Bennet?"

"She was a short, very showy blonde; just had two or three lines in the whole play. A gorgeous girl, really. She was at Mike's party. She wore a bright red dress. I saw you speak to her once, Sandy; she was with someone you seemed to know."

Suddenly I remembered the blonde Johnnie had been busy with all evening. "Of course, I know now—the blonde in the red dress. And that was Joyce Bennet?"

"That's Joyce Bennet. She was in father's office just this morning, and when she found out that we blamed Floyd, she almost fainted. I happened to be there, getting some money from father, and I helped her get straightened out and finally I took her home in a cab. She lives at the Hotel Sandringham, on 58th Street, just off the Avenue." Lisa's face sobered and she frowned. "When I got her into bed, I went tip-toeing around her living room. There was a large picture of Floyd Harvey, inscribed and autographed. 'With Love.' I talked to her for a while, and said I'd be back to see how she was, later tonight. We got to talking, and she said she was mainly upset over Floyd's disappearance, not Mike's! I asked her why so? She said that Floyd and she had been going to get married as soon as Martha got her divorce. Floyd, it seems, didn't have the money for a divorce, but Martha was going to finance the project."

"Did she tell you anything more?"

"Only one thing. She told me that she was terribly afraid that they'd blame the whole thing on Floyd, because Floyd had told her that he hated Michael, couldn't bear him, and would do anything to hurt the show. Joyce felt that if Floyd Harvey had told her that much, he must have told some of the others, and someone would be

75

certain to put the blame on him, which is just what happened!"

"I'm going up there when you go," I interrupted. "All right?"

Lisa smiled. "That's one reason why I was so glad you asked me to dinner."

"I ought to have interviewed the whole cast, right away," I mused with self-blame, but Lisa made a small moue.

"Not necessarily," Lisa continued. "People outside the theater somehow always have the idea that everyon on the stage knows everyone else. More often than not the people hired in any play have never seen one another before, and may never see one another again. You wouldn't get much, I don't believe, from any of the cast."

"You got quite a lot from Joyce Bennet," I countered.

"That was a coincidence," she remarked. "We'll go as soon as I finish my coffee."

We finished with coffee and a liquer, and as Lisa sipped her brandy I stared into her eyes.

"Lisa," I demanded firmly, "those letters in the pink ribbon that disappeared from Mike's safe. I want to know what they are."

Her eyes widened, until at last she stammered, "I don't know, honestly-. . . honestly, Sandy. I don't know what they were."

"Why did you take them? They were Michael's, weren't they?"

For a long moment she did not answer, then her voice was strangely strained. "That's why I took them, Sandy. One day Michael showed me that bundle of old letters. He said that if anything happened to him I was to take them right away, and keep them for him. It was the day he moved from the old apartment. He gave me a key to the Park Avenue place and when he disappeared . . . well, I went there . . ."

"Lisa," I said softly, "I want to read those letters. Will you give them to me?"

There was a moment's electric silence, then her refusal came, stifled and low. "I can't, Sandy—I can't let you read them."

"Why, Lisa?"

"I burned them."

"And you don't know what was in those letters at all?" I asked tensely. "Did Mike order you to burn them?"

She slowly nodded her graceful head. "He told me to burn them," she repeated somnambulistically. "That's all I know about them."

"Well, I'll be damned," I said, appraising her. "I wish I had someone who would look after my interests like that." I helped her into her coat, and we went into the cold air of Greenwich Village.

As we stood before the restaurant, Lisa turned to me.

"If we're going up to Joyce Bennet's, I think I ought to call her first," she informed me, and turned back into the *Jumble Shop*.

Standing there waiting for her, I analyzed this last revelation, intended obviously to put a stop to the matter of the letters. Lisa had burned them, and had told me she did not know what was in them. I loved Lisa, I admitted it to myself; but not for one second did I believe her. She *must* have known what was in those letters. It was beyond human belief that she did not. For Mike had loved her, and still did; he had finally entrusted to her the letters which I had no doubt must have been of tremendous importance to him, whether he had stolen them or not. In the dim cold of the late Fall, I felt the mystery of Michael Rawn thicken and collect about me once again. I surmised that Michael had spent a long time searching for those letters, that they had belonged to his long-dead past, and once he had found them it was most important to Mike that they stay in his hands or in those of one most dear to him. Yet within a week after his disappearance, those all-important letters had been burned. It was impossible. A frightening conjecture assailed me. Had my friend, Michael Rawn, been kidnapped by someone who knew or guessed that he found the letters at last; who also wanted them; who could not know of Michael's bequest to Lisa?

At this instant she returned to my side at the curb.

"Joyce Bennet is entertaining a date," she reported, "but he'll be gone in about half an hour. We can put in the time till then, can't we?"

I took her arm. "It's a privilege and a pleasure, Miss Cushman," I smiled. Although hurt by her story of the letters, there was nothing I could do, so I determined to make the best of a bad situation.

We taxied up Fifth Avenue as far as 34th Street, and then decided that by walking the rest of the way we would just about kill the rest of the half-hour. We window-shopped as we went, and I got quite a belt out of pretending to myself that Lisa Cushman and I were married, and were out for a nice, connubial walk—just a young couple strolling through the autumn evening. I knew I was day-dreaming, that sooner or later I must discover the end of the puzzle of Michael Rawn, that my foolish bubble would burst, and that I'd be right back where I started, keeping house with John Olds in the West 70's.

At last we turned the corner at Bergdorf-Goodman's and walked west to the Hotel Sandringham. Joyce Bennet's apartment was on the second floor, and we walked up without giving our names. The door was standing ajar. A light from the living room fell across the carpet in the hall. I knocked, turning to Lisa.

"Did you tell her you were bringing a friend?"

"Yes," Lisa whispered, "I told her you were interested in anything she could tell you about Floyd Harvey. She said to come right up when we got here."

I knocked again. Finally Lisa pushed the door open, calling, "Miss Bennet, it's Lisa Cushman . . . Joyce?"

There was no answer, so we went in. Lisa turned to me. "Sit down, Sandy. She's probably downstairs ordering something to drink."

We waited a minute, then Lisa rose and knocked on the door to the bedroom. The two rooms adjoined. There was no answer, and Lisa looked around at me. "Do you suppose we should wait?"

"Why not? She expects us." We sat down again and prepared to wait for Joyce Bennet.

We had chatted aimlessly for about three or four minutes, when I glanced at the door to the bedroom again. All at once my heart beat like a trip-hammer. The carpet of the living room was pale tan. Onto it, coming from under the bedroom door, was seeping slowly a finger of dark, wet ooze. Lisa saw it almost when I did.

"Sandy . . ." She came and took my arm.

I freed myself and went to the bedroom door. It was closed, but not locked. I pushed it open, then turned to motion Lisa away.

"Get over on that sofa," I ordered roughly. She went, propelled by my tone. I stared down at my feet.

Joyce Bennet had tried to get out of the room. She was lying face down on the floor, her head about two feet from the door to the living room. On the back of her neck was a dark welt. It had not caused her death.

She had struggled to escape; the half-sleeve of her dinner dress was torn. Her assailant had caught and held her. Joyce Bennet had died immediately, her face blown off by a pistol held at very close range.

CHAPTER TWELVE

With the murder of Joyce Bennet, the newspapers launched a wild man-hunt, led by the *Globe*. My name began to appear in a by-line, and editors all over the country demanded my now-syndicated stories. Pat Curry was pleased, and gave me a raise in pay. But while

78

my added prestige put me in solid at the *Globe* Building, I discovered that it left me entangled in the same grinding confusion as before.

Although I was very careful to keep the word "alleged" well forward in the theories I set up, Pat Curry urged me to put direct pressure on the search for the understudy, Floyd Harvey. As a result, papers in New York declared outright for his capture. There seemed little reason to hold fire, and I found my personal search for Michael Rawn fading. The sensational twin killings of the glamorous actresses, both beautiful, had horrified and frightened New Yorkers and captured the interest of the nation. Floyd Harvey was described openly as a double killer and kidnapper, and while the police, through Dan Cassidy, assured me that they were still on the prowl for Mike, I eventually got the feeling that the hunt was more for a trace of Floyd Harvey than for a missing star called Michael Rawn.

But my loneliness was of the spirit; physically I had never been busier. Phone calls swamped my desk; one switchboard girl was detailed to take only my calls. Hundreds of people were phoning in clues, long distance collect and otherwise. Floyd Harvey was seen in Battery, Nyack, and Hoboken; in Gimbel's Basement and Birmingham. Young girls turned up claiming to be his wife, his mistress, his long-lost daughter, and one old tat, whiskey on her breath, said she was his dear lost mother, that they had gotten separated in the San Francisco earthquake, and how much did he leave?

Through it all, the same old feeling of cloudy, miserable vagueness enveloped me. I wrote my stories, Pat Curry took them and rushed them into print, Johnnie was assigned to help me in any way he could, and we spent days tracking down every tip we got, feeling that they would prove fruitless, as eventually all did. Desperate, I continued to interview everyone and anyone—the cast of Mike's play, once again Mrs. Martin and Mr. Sam Cushman, who was readying another drama for production. I searched the apartment on 88th Street again, as well as the apartments of Joyce Bennet and Martha Wain. Dan Cassidy was in a fury of work on the Bennet killing, and, perhaps out of some new respect for my prestige in the newspaper world, perhaps out of his own befuddlement, told me whatever he discovered.

Together or separately, we were four-star duds. As the days went past I knew, with increasing conviction, that we were getting nowhere. I had found no further trace of Michael Rawn, the police had not found Floyd Harvey. There had been no actual clues in Joyce Bennet's murder; we had found no gun, no fingerprints—nothing. With a growing sense of panic, I realized that when the sensation of the double murder faded and public hysteria begar to die, Pat Curry would lift me off the Michael Rawn case and put me onto the next crime. I became dyspnoic before the crushing pressure of inexorable time. Soon, if I were to continue hunting Michael, I *had* to find something.

I came back to the apartment from the office one morning at 3:00 a. m., dead beat. I had written two features, recalling facts from the early life of Michael Rawn, reviewing the story of the party and the double disappearance of Michael and the understudy, and felt that now I had written the very last word that could be pumped out of the case, without some new discovery. Throwing my coat on the floor in disgust, I flopped into a chair. Johnnie came to stand over me, frowning. My worry had infected him.

"Still nothing new?" he asked, half-hopefully.

I shook my head disconsolately. "Not one damn thing."

"What are you going to do, Sandy?"

"What the hell *can* I do? I'm hired by Pat Curry; either I find something to keep going or he puts me on something else, that's all!"

Johnnie handed me his drink from the top of the bureau. "Here, take a noseful of this," he said. "Maybe you'll think of something."

"Hell,", I exploded, "I've thought of everything I've got brains for . . ."

Johnnie filled his pipe, dragged a chair over beside mine, and began very quietly. "I was thinking, Sandy; just tonight. You've been close, working too hard with the features and all. Maybe it's been easier for me. Listen to this . . ."

I perked up. I might as well give ear. Johnnie might have something. "What's your idea?"

He smiled deprecatingly. "Well, it sounds simple, but why don't we try to discover just what we would do, where we would hide, if we were killing Martha Wain and Joyce Bennet, then had to disappear, like Harvey has done."

"Why not?" I assented apathetically. "We've done everything else."

Johnnie warmed to his thesis. "Don't forget; where we're hiding has to be a place that we can keep Mike in some safety, too."

I nodded. The newspapers and the police agreed, that since the body of Michael Rawn had not been discovered, he must still be in captivity somewhere.

"Go ahead, killer," I urged, "What would you do? You've

killed two women and got to hide the hottest bundle in town—a kidnapped stage star."

"Well," he started lengthily, "I'd get out of town. I certainly wouldn't try to stay in Manhattan, where people knew me . . ."

"That's right, at that." I sat up. "The hunt is all over the country, but only in Manhattan could anyone identify you and your prisoner very easily." •

Johnnie stared at the floor, continuing, "Frankly, I'd just lay low. I wouldn't do anything. I already have Mike's dough, I have Mike, the only living witness against me, and I've killed the two women who could tell anything—and I've got away with it! I'd be pretty hard to find because I'd just sit tight; never move!".

"You're right," I admitted. "If you just keep quiet you'd be comparatively safe." I went on more quietly, "And now that you're sitting pretty, with Mike lashed to a chair, with safety and money on your side, just what would you do with Michael Rawn?"

"After the hue and cry died down; I'd have to kill him," John whispered with finality.

"Nothing to it!" I mocked, and we dropped into a silence. All at once I catapulted from my chair. "JOHNNIE! I've an idea! Why the hell didn't we think of it before!"

He stared at me wide-eyed. "Don't scare me like that! What it is, for God's sake?"

"Well," I reminded him, "you'd get away from Manhattan if you were the killer, you said. What is the first thing you'd have to do? I'll tell you—*you'd have to buy a railroad ticket.*"

"Cassidy watched the stations," Johnnie reminded me.

"Yes, but I want to go down myself and talk to them. Get your coat on!"

Well, it had been a good idea, we allowed, when we finished a disappointing session at Grand Central Terminal. The supervisors had been wonderfully cooperative, but so many people went past the ticket windows that unless the sellers were on the qui vive, people's individualities went unnoticed.

Our second try was the supervisor of ticket sellers at Pennsylvania Station. We had less hope at Penn, because we felt Floyd Harvey would hide in a close point, somewhere on the New Haven, upper New York or Connecticut. Mr. Leo Gunster, the supervisor, was ready for us. We had called him from the Grand Central when we had fizzled there.

"Mr. Blunt," he stated, "I couldn't be certain, but we may have something of interest for you. It's difficult to explain."

"Don't try, Mr. Gunster," I declared, "I'm only too glad to have your cooperation. What do you think you have to tell me?"

"We have three girls who would like to speak to you," he continued somewhat nervously. "Of course, they may not all . . ."

"May I talk to them one at a time, Mr. Gunster?"

He left his office, and in a minute the door opened and Mr. Gunster announced in clarion tones, "Miss Cadick!"

Miss Cadick applied her lipstick and took a chair after the manner of a movie divorcee, casting her eyes lushly upon Johnnie, who grinned back at her.

"All right, Miss Cadick."

"Well," she began, "I'm just minding my own business, one night last week, and this man comes to my window; a ticket for Elkhart, Indiana, he wants. So he . . ."

"What did this man look like?"

"Well, he was short, with light hair, kind of curly . . . and . . ."

I took a picture out of a breast pocket. "Is this the man who bought a ticket from you?"

She nodded at once. "That's the one . . ."

I replaced the picture. "Thank you very much, Miss Cadick." She left, with a languishing glance for John Olds. I looked up at John and we shared a look. The picture was one I had got from Cassidy; an old photograph of a killer, dead in Sing-Sing. I had found good use for it in derailing notoriety-seekers in the past weeks.

"Next," John Olds said to Mr. Gunster, who stuck his head in as Miss Cadick left. An attractive girl, classified loosely as "the business type" came in as Miss Cadick left.

"Miss Walsh," declared Mr. Gunster, shutting the door behind her.

She had her notes on a piece of paper; got off to a swift start by firmly denying the picture of the killer, and looking at me coldly when she had done so.

"Mr. Blunt," she directed, "I'll tell you as much as I can so don't try to put me off with pictures; I know what I'm doing." I nodded apologetically.

"Fine, Miss Walsh; now what did your customer look like?"

"You may think it peculiar that I wrote it all down," she preambled, "but I get bored working all night, and I keep copies of the tabloids and the society columns, just to see if I ever get any of the photographed people for customers. Well, just six days ago tonight this man came in to buy a ticket for Pittsburgh. He was about five feet six or seven, I guess, blue eyes, somewhat square-jawed, and he had a short crewcut. I think he is the man the newspapers are hunting."

"Why didn't you get in touch with the police, Miss Walsh?"

"I told them what I'm telling you, Mr. Blunt. They said they'd look into it; but I never heard any more." I cursed Dan Cassidy under my breath; holding out something that might be important. I reached out and shook her hand.

"Miss Walsh, you've done me a great favor . . ." She nodded firmly and left. Johnnie slapped me on the back.

"Well . . ." he exulted, "she saw Floyd Harvey all right!"

I was almost afraid to believe what Miss Walsh had told me; it was the purest kind of luck that she had been sharp. But before I went any further I picked up the phone and called Dan Cassidy.

"Yea?"

"Listen, Inspector, this is Sandy Blunt. What about this business of Miss Walsh at Penn Station? I'm here now, and she said she told you about Floyd Harvey buying a ticket for Pittsburgh."

"Sandy, my boy, there's nothing to it, take my word for it! The girl is a good girl, but it so happens that we have just ten ticket sellers all over the country who say they sold tickets to Floyd Harvey. I've had everyone in the country who sells railroad tickets investigated completely. There's nothing in it; take it from me! Harvey is hiding Mike Rawn right here in this town, if only we could find the devil's hide of him."

"Yes, but have you tried to trace this ticket to Pittsburgh? Remember the ticket I gave you that I found in Martha Wain's pocketbook?"

"Ah, and don't I?" he mourned loudly, "with you holding it up for a day or so until I got it? Well, I do remember Pittsburgh at that; Martha Wain . . . . spawn of the devil all of them . . ." his Gaelic emphasis toned to a low boom. "Well, and now maybe you have something there, at that, Sandy. I'll try to get hold of the conductors on the train. Maybe they can tell me something, and if you find out any more, let me know? I'll do all I can; and no crooked business any more like that ticket of Martha Wain's, you understand?"

I smiled. Cassidy had smarted over that ticket considerably, and had not permitted me to forget it. "All right, Cassidy, and no holding out on me . . . OK?"

"Ah," he mourned, "as if we could fall out . . . me as what made you the fine newspaperman that you are."

We closed on a note of mutual amity and watchful neutrality. Johnnie had put on his coat, and was holding mine.

"You won't want to talk to the other girl," he presumed. "She must be another one of those gals who longs to have her picture in the papers."

I took my coat from him, and inquired, "All right, John, this was your idea! Now what would you do, now that you've bought a ticket for Pittsburgh, where no one knows you? You know the police everywhere are looking for you, so where can you hide? Certainly you don't think hiding is going to be any easier in Pittsburgh than it is in New York?"

Johnnie sat down on the edge of a desk, thinking. Mr. Gunster popped in and asked, "Are you ready to speak to Miss Douglas, Mr. Blunt?"

There was a pause, then I said, "Just a minute, Mr. Gunster." He jerked his head in understanding, and closed the door.

"Well?" I asked Johnnie half-derisively.

He made a face and threw up his hands. "I'm stuck. If the police can't find Floyd Harvey in Pittsburgh, I can't do any more for them," John laughed. "Hell, Sandy, you know how to do these things—it's natural to you."

"Let's go, it's late," I concluded, shrugging into my coat. At the door we were met by Mr. Gunster, who was ushering in a small stout girl, with bright brown eyes, and I faced the combination wearily.

"Mr. Blunt, I would like to present Miss Rita Douglas. She is the third young lady who thinks she has something of importance to tell you."

Miss Douglas looked beseechingly at me, and Johnnie sat down again, rolling his eyes ceilingward in boredom. With a sigh, I took out my Sing-Sing picture.

"All right, Miss Douglas, is this the man you claim to have seen?"

"No," she replied almost inaudibly.

"What did your customer buy from you?" I was suddenly very tired, and my voice took on a half-scornful inflection.

"He bought a drawing room to Chicago." She recognized my mood, and seemed to retreat within herself.

Johnnie shared a helpless look with me, but Mr. Gunster, admitted to the audience at last, was beaming. He had cooperated, and he should have his money's worth, I decided.

"Why do you remember this particular man?" I inquired.

"Well, my window is next to Miss Walsh's and I often use the papers, just like she does, for the fun of it. I don't often see anyone I recognize, because she only gives me the papers when they get old, but anyway, that same night Miss Walsh sold her ticket . . ."

I sighed deeply; another repeat performance, a road company of Miss Walsh's admirable tactics. I was sick to death of pretenders; I didn't know the whole world was so full of them.

"You sold a ticket to the blond man, too, Miss Douglas?" I was prepared to discover that Floyd Harvey had bought a ticket to Chicago as a blind; her answer nearly knocked me down.

"No," Rita Douglas insisted quietly. "My Chicago drawing room was sold to another man, about half-an-hour later . . ." she hesitated apologetically. "He was small, and kind of thin and pale, with sort of sad eyes. But mostly I remember his hair. It was darkish, but a strange color of red . . ."

CHAPTER THIRTEEN

I was up at ten the next morning, and went down to talk with Dan Cassidy. He was eating a belated breakfast when I arrived at his office.

"Ah, it's you, is it?" He hailed me sourly. "A worthless spalpeen, if ever I seen one. After I practically make you the *Globe's* best you have to blame me for laxity and God-knows-what and a phone call in the middle of the night along with it!"

"Yes," I admitted, "but what did you do about it? Someone has to keep the Great Cassidy on his toes!"

"What did I do about it! Well, me fine young bucko, there was a detail off and away to Pittsburgh within the hour of your call, that's what old Dan Cassidy did about it! Them Pittsburgh police cooperate like nobody's business!"

"Make any finds on the railroad end?"

"Sure I did, if finds you could call them," he continued dourly. "It's a plain case of suicide, if you ask me! Everything we have is a blind alley. But this much I did get. The ticket the short-haired blond man bought was a coach seat to Pittsburg, and it can't be traced.

There's a thousand like it sold every twenty-four hours. But," Cassidy pointed a dramatic finger at me, ". . . but what does our red-headed friend, who ought by rights to be dead this long time—what does he do but buy this drawing room . . . and never use it!"

"Never use it!"

"Right! And I said myself that the case of this Rawn ought to be closed. He's by right a missing person by this time, and no care of ours."

I felt a sweat of desperation crawl over me. "Cassidy! You've got lots to do! What about the drawing room to Chicago?"

He nodded judicially, pulling his mouth down at the corners. "Everything! The drawing room was never occupied. The ticket was never collected; whoever bought it just never got on the train, is my guess. The Pullman conductor told me the drawing room rode the whole way without a soul in it!"

"Well, Michael Rawn is alive! It must have been Mike who bought that ticket!" I was excited and sounded it.

Cassidy shook his head slowly but firmly. "It must have been; you can say it if you like, me boy. But I talked myself with this same conductor, and he remembers no one like that on the whole train."

We stared at each other for a moment; I said slowly, as though reading a thought that ran through both our minds, *"Then he's gone a second time. Michael Rawn has disappeared again!"*

"Like a banshee himself," Cassidy agreed seriously.

I thanked him, and after extracting a promise to let me know if he got onto a new line, I went to the *Globe* office. I told Pat Curry about the drawing room to Chicago that Michael had ostensibly bought, finishing by pointing out that this was the second time Michael Rawn had disappeared from a public place, filled with people any of whom could have recognized him.

Pat Curry slanted a glance at my worried face. "Don't forget, Blunt, that somewhere right near Michael Rawn must have been Harvey, our short-haired friend. Rawn was probably being covered with a gun all the time he was forced to buy that ticket. He couldn't have called out or made a break, and he knew it!"

"That's right, at that," I admitted grudgingly. I sat down and tore out a short feature on it, excluding the names of the girls who had been interviewed. Then I went home. Johnnie was painting a small sketch on beaverboard.

We ruminated over salami on rye. Michael had walked up to a

ticket window in the biggest railroad station in the world, had calmly bought a ticket and once again had vanished like mist! But, I considered, Cassidy was right. Everyone in the station would be going about his business; it was understandable that no one remembered Michael, even with the big play the papers had given his story. It had been mere chance and the sharp eyes of the two ticket-sellers that had given us as much information as we had. The night Joyce Bennet had been murdered, Floyd Harvey must have decided that New York was too hot a place for him and his captive, so that same night he had planned to move Mike Rawn out of town. Therefore the tickets. But logical as it was, there was a terrible fallacy. Only one of the tickets seemed to have been used! I mentioned this to Johnnie. He shrugged.

"That's only what any smart criminal would do," he instructed. "He made Mike buy the drawing room ticket for a blind. Then Floyd, who wouldn't let Mike out of his sight for an instant, got someone standing in line to buy him another ticket, a coach ticket for Pittsburgh, or wherever he meant to take Mike. Hell, we don't know it was Pittsburgh they really went to!"

"Right," I conformed to his opinion. "Still, there's something fiendish about this."

"About what? The Pittsburgh tickets?"

"Yes, the Pittsburgh tickets," I echoed. "For a minute those tickets made me forget something that must be important—perhaps one of the biggest things in the case."

"What's that?"

"Why, that room up on 88th Street, with the clothes Mike was wearing when he left the theater the night he disappeared." I ticked off on my fingers, "The blood under the carpet. Mike's clothes in that room. Don't you see, Johnnie. Something has gone on in that room. Something must have!" I squared my jaw. "I might as well tell you; I thought that room was the place where Floyd Harvey had taken Mike. I thought he had killed Mike there. But no one's been in that room for almost two weeks!"

"For that matter, we don't know for certain whether or not Floyd Harvey is the killer," he maintained. "Just because he disappears doesn't mean he did all this. It would be the perfect cover-up for a third party who really wanted to kill Michael. This third party could kill them both, and we'd be no wiser than we are right now."

I shook my head. "But they've *both* been seen! And if Floyd

Harvey is innocent, he'd show up. He'd have come out of hiding before this. And killing two just to be certain of getting one sounds too difficult to me. Who would take such a long chance?"

"Well," Johnnie swallowed the end of his sandwich, "you've done everything anyone could do for Mike. The police in every city in the country are hunting for Floyd Harvey. That baby can't get far, that's a sure thing."

"God knows I'm screwed in a loop," I muttered despondently. "I don't have any notion of what to do next. I've got to find Mike or go crazy; that's all I know."

There was a pause, deeper and longer. Johnnie broke it to inquire, "Did you ever hear from that Valerian, who phoned you?"

"I tried to get in touch with him; but some servant said he was out of town—for a month, if you have time."

Johnnie filled a glass with milk. "Well, then, there doesn't seem much more you can do but wait," he said, his lips tightened.

"Well," I grunted, "I've got two more steps to take and then I'll admit I'm licked. I'll talk to Mr. Sam Cushman once more; and take a shot at my old friend, Miss Jasmine Le Valley, though I swear to God I don't know what I expect them to tell me!"

"I'd like to paint Le Valley," Johnnie grinned.

"I'll bet you would; paint her red—all over—but wait until I get through with questions before you proposition La Belle Le Valley."

"What are you so eager to talk to her again for—a tease?"

I ignored the insinuation loftily. "Listen, my crummy chum, you see before you a man of tears and sorrows. Hell, there isn't a good lust in me any more. I'm a machine for muckraking."

Another pause fell into our banter, and Johnnie said seriously, "You insist those missing letters were Mike's own?"

"Yes. He must have hunted them for years. I think frankly that when he found them, his troubles began."

"What would the letters have to do with it?"

"Hell, that's just one of the things I have to find out; how—don't ask me! But I think Jasmine Le Valley, the last person to possess them before Mike got them—I think she can tell me."

Just then the phone rang. It was Lisa; her voice sounded cool and heavenly.

"Yes. Is it really you, Lisa?"

She laughed, a lovely sound. "Yes. I've read your last stories, Sandy; they're wonderful." I thanked her, and she went on. "I'd like you to take me to dinner again, Sandy—tonight. Will you?"

"I'd like to," I understated, then hesitated. As she did not hang up or go on, I prompted, "Did you have something particular to tell me, Lisa?"

She took a deep breath, and I felt decision in her slow answer. "Yes, Sandy, I do. Those letters you asked about. Well, Sandy, I want to talk to you about them. So does father. After dinner we'll go up to his office."

"I thought you burned them."

"I had to lie to you, Sandy. You'll have to forgive me; I thought I had a reason."

"What has your father got to do with them?"

"I can't talk to you about the letters now, Sandy. I've got to see you, please. Please, Sandy."

I smiled; Lisa never had to say please to me in that tone. "I didn't mean to cross-examine, Lisa. I'd like nothing better than to have you to dinner. Shall I call for you?"

"No," she responded, "I'll meet you on the Fifth Avenue end of the Promenade at the Center. Make it about seven."

I hung up, mystified at what could have happened to make Lisa suddenly want to come into the open about the letters. It was strange enough that she had lied to me about them, but now her father seemed somehow involved. As I recalled the day after Mike's disappearance, I cursed the impulse that had kept me from reading those letters when they had lain on the writing desk before me. I had paid dearly for my false sense of delicacy.

Before I left the apartment for Rockefeller Center, I phoned Dan Cassidy and asked him if he had any news from the Pittsburgh police. He had. No trace of Floyd Harvey having stopped in Pittsburgh at all.

I waited where the Promenade meets Fifth until almost half-past seven. I had almost decided to give up and phone Lisa when I heard a voice at my elbow.

"Need a date, Handsome?"

I whirled around and looked into Lisa's amused violet eyes. She laughed as I took her arm, and we started back toward the Plaza.

"Is that how you let yourself get picked up, Sandy?"

"I'm fussy," I answered her, "I only go out with my girl if she asks my mother how long she can keep me out."

89

"How about me? Right now you didn't seem hard to get." '

"You're not my girl ; . ." It was out before I realized what I had said.

Lisa's face sobered, and she repeated quietly, "No, Sandy; I'm not your girl . . ."

We reached the restaurant and were silent until we were seated and gave our order. Then I asked, "What did you want to tell me?"

Lisa bit her lip, as though deciding how to begin, then looked full into my face. I got that catch in the solar plexus again, but kept my eyes on hers.

"I'll get right into it, Sandy," she started. "I have never known about those letters. But I didn't burn them; I gave them to someone else. Mike asked me to take them, all right; but I took them to someone who wanted them."

"Who sent for them—who got them, anyway?"

She put a hand over mine. "Sandy, don't look like that. No one sent me for them; but I gave them to someone after I had them. I did what I thought was best. I didn't know."

"Lisa, whoever sent you for those letters was gambling with your life. I think Martha Wain and Joyce Bennet and Mike himself have been . . . those letters must be at the bottom of all of this!"

She seemed startled for a minute, then continued, her voice low. "Maybe, Sandy, but I was the only person who knew the combination of the safe outside of Biglow. And . . . Sandy, I had to have those letters!"

"Did you write them?"

Lisa shook her head. "No, Sandy, I didn't write them. I told you I don't know what was in them for certain. I could guess."

"What is in them? Lisa, for God's sake . . ."

"I can't tell you, Sandy. But I think father can. That is why I wanted to see you tonight. To explain myself . . . my part in taking those letters you seem to need so badly."

"All right, Lisa. Who asked you for the letters? Where are they now?"

Lisa was silent for a moment as the waiter put down our plates of food. Neither of us touched a morsel. "Mr. Valerian sent me to get the letters. He told me what they looked like."

"Mr. Valerian!" I could not hide my shock and surprise. "What the hell had Mr. Valerian to do with Mike's letters?"

"I don't exactly know, Sandy. He told me to take them to father.

Mr. Valerian and father are acquainted, but I never thought they were very friendly. But Mr. Valerian talked to me the day after Mike vanished. He said the letters were important to *me* as well as to Mike. That's all he'd tell me. When I took them to father, father knew about them, and he took them from me. He keeps them in his office. I persuaded him to talk to you about them; I said you had been hunting them."

"Does Mr. Valerian know what is in the letters?"

"Yes; he must."

"Why did you do what he said, Lisa?"

She shrugged. "At the time it seemed all right. No one else seemed to want them. I was Michael's fiancee; there was no reason I shouldn't have them. Mike had told me to take them if . . . anything happened to him. He spoke to Biglow about them; then I guess he felt they'd be safer if I took them. I know he talked to me *after* he mentioned them to Biglow."

"Did Mr. Valerian know Michael?" I demanded.

"Mr. Valerian knew him very well."

"It's a damn funny thing he hasn't come forward with what he knows. I phoned him once, after he had tried to reach me twice, and he was out of town on a vacation!"

She said nothing, just looked at me. Finally I collected myself. "And where are the letters right now? In your father's safe?"

"Yes," Lisa replied, "up in father's office."

"Who is *he* keeping them for? The police would like to see them. There's a word called 'collusion,' Lisa, and it's a damned ugly one."

She paled and looked at me. "Sandy, it's cost me more than you know to come to you with this story. I don't know how you'll feel about me after this. But the story isn't mine. Father can tell you what you want to know. Please don't be too hard on me."

I smiled wryly. "Sorry, Lisa. I love having dinner with you; you know I do. Excuse me for being such lousy company. I know what it costs you—with Mike missing and all."

But even though I tried to lift our spirits as dinner went on, something had fallen between us. We finished our coffee in silence. At last Lisa rose.

"Ready to go?" She consulted her watch. "Father will be waiting for us."

Silently I paid the check, and we left, walking slowly to the Fifth Avenue entrance of her father's building. In the elevator my heart lifted with excitement. I had followed those letters of Mike's a long, devious path. Now—but why did Mr. Sam Cushman have Mike's letters in his safe? Why did he trust so implicitly the word of the mysterious Mr. Valerian, painter and dilettant? Why did he permit Lisa to go to Mike's apartment on the advice of the unknown Valerian, as a dangerous courier for those much-sought-after letters?

The granite hall was dark; no light in the Cushman Productions front office either. The door was slightly ajar! I pushed it open for Lisa and we passed through the ghosts of the modern office furniture, gaunt and black in the silence. The door into Mr. Cushman's private office was of padded, tufted leather. Lisa swung it open and we stepped inside—and were confronted by a macabre sight.

The big desk faced the door. Behind it, facing us squarely, sat Sam Cushman, staring at us. The light from a lamp made his face a mask. He did not move. We stood transfixed for a second; Lisa gave a quavering cry and ran toward him, I behind her. We lifted him to a sofa on one side of the room, and I listened at his chest. There was a faint, but steady, beat. On the back of Sam Cushman's head was a growing welt, large; but the skin had not been broken. Lisa swabbed his forehead with water from the cooler, while I phoned the watchman and Cassidy, after which I turned my attention to a big open safe, facing the room near the desk.

The contents were strewn in complete disorder onto the floor before the safe. I fumbled through the mess. Those letters—they *must* be here. Yet I knew I would not find them. I rose to my feet, sick at heart, looking down at the tangle of contracts, leases, small empty clamps for papers. I cursed softly, roundly, feelingly; and stooped to detach something that had stuck to the sole of my shoe.

It was an old, soiled, pink ribbon.

I held it up to Lisa, and she nodded, once. A look satisfied me that her father was coming round. Then a small sound riveted my attention. I met Lisa's eyes. They were wide with fear. We looked toward the outer office. *The door into the outer office was closing!*

I rushed it; it slammed in my face, and I heard a key flip over in the lock. It was a thick door, and I heaved against it in vain.

Footsteps, determined but unhurried, passed through the room beyond and went down the hall.

CHAPTER FOURTEEN

It was the next evening before Mr. Sam Cushman could tell what had happened to him. It was simple and definitive, and helped not at all.

He had gone to his office, leaving the outer door open, as he recalled it; had gone directly into his private office, and smoked a cigarette. As the time came for Lisa and me to join him, he had opened the safe, and begun to extract the letters and some other papers he had wanted to look over while he waited for us. He had knelt down before the safe with his back to the room, and as the safe creaked open, he had heard hurrying foosteps. As he looked around, something cracked down on his skull, and he had become unconscious. When he came to, we had found him. That, in brief, was all he could tell of what had happened.

I stood by his bedside while Dan Cassidy questioned Sam Cushman. It occurred to me that now that Cushman knew the letters had been stolen from him, he had decided not to talk about them. He repeated that he knew nothing. I caught Lisa's eye once, but there was no glimmer of response. She was going along with her father. But hurt though he might be, Sam Cushman's replies to Dan Cassidy's questions were short and pointed.

"No, I don't know why the letters would be stolen . . . I don't know who struck me, or what reason he might have outside of burglary . . . I did not see my assailant . . . I can think of no reason . . ."

And so it went. The damage had been done, and now Mr. Sam Cushman, out of fear or for some reason of his own, refused to be of any help. At last he asked the attendant doctor if he might be left alone with his daughter, and we were asked out of the room.

I walked to the elevator with Cassidy.

"Well, Inspector?"

Cassidy shook his head. "A lot of messing around about nothing. I've put out the net for that Floyd Harvey, and he's been trouble enough as it is! He may buy railroad tickets, but he sticks pretty close. Sure they can do what they like about their letters, for all of me. Once I can get a hand on that young spalpeen of a Harvey, I've got my man."

"What about the missing Michael Rawn?"

Cassidy looked at me with something akin to pity. "Well, me boy, he was your good friend, and a fine youngster that Rawn must have been—and right promising at that—but if I was you, I'd put it out of me mind."

I stopped. "Listen, Cassidy, you know me. Now what is it? What do they think down at Headquarters? There is something I'm not getting from you. What is it?"

He hesitated a minute, then looked at me with his weather-beaten Irish face. "Well, Sandy lad, I guess it would be better that I tell you straight off, at that. Headquarters has given up Mike Rawn for lost. They're hunting for Floyd Harvey himself. The idea is that Harvey has done something with the body of this other young man— this friend of yours."

"You mean they've called off the drag-net?"

"They have that. We get the reports from the police offices all over the country, but they ain't hoping for a living man any more, son."

We entered the elevator in silence. It was the first time I felt completely alone in the disappearance of Mike. They had given him up. They thought from what had happened to Wain and Bennet, that Mike was surely dead. I felt the idea hit me like a ton of brick. It was true. I had not admitted it to myself, but the logic of it was irrefutable. Somewhere, perhaps in this city, the body of Michael Rawn was hidden.

With a surge of terrible hatred I thought of the two times I had been so near the killer. The view of the running figure I had caught from the roof of the theater the night I had been so nearly killed; and last night, when Lisa and I had been locked so neatly into Cushman's private office to allow the killer to escape. I had not the least doubt that the same killer had come for Sam Cushman as had previously visited Joyce Bennet, and before that Martha Wain. And there could be no quiver of doubt that because of my writing, the killer was not adverse to taking a shot at me in passing. I had played right into his hands the night I visited Mike's theater.

I left Cassidy and took a cab down to the office. Pat Curry glanced up as I sat on the corner of his desk.

"Well, Blunt, what's on your mind?"

"I want the straight dope, Curry," I declared. "I want to know what you actually think about the Mike Rawn affair. Maybe I've been too close to it; but today Cassidy tells me that Headquarters has given up looking for Mike. They want Floyd Harvey, and that's all."

Pat put his head to one side.

"Listen, Sandy," he said smoothly, "this is getting at your nerves.

I'll tell you frankly how I feel. I agree with Cassidy. I think myself, knowing what I do about criminals, that Mike Rawn is dead as a doornail. Hell, boy, he's *got* to be; Floyd Harvey couldn't take the risks that keeping him alive would involve! Frankly, I think your friend Rawn was murdered and the body hidden some time shortly after Floyd got hold of Rawn's money."

"Then why haven't we got a body? Why don't the dumb cops hunt for that body?"

He stood up. "They are. Harvey's just been too clever for them. I think you're letting this get you. You've given this thing a full coverage, Blunt. I want you to take a little vacation, anywhere you like. Put it on your expense account. Take a couple of days off. You're going stale on it."

I shook my head. "Not right away. I want to know *from you* if I can go ahead on this Rawn thing on my own? I mean, I don't have to follow the police . . ."

He waved his hand. "Hell, boy, I'd be glad if you found Michael Rawn. The only thing is; he *must be dead*—he's got to be! You're wasting your time . . . but do what you want to do so far as the story is concerned. You're doing all right. But you need to get the hell out of town for a few days."

"Thanks a lot. I may take you up on it." The starch and the fury were leaving me now, leaving me with that sense of aching foreboding, that sense of being cornered, blocked off from what I should know. With a sigh I phoned the Rose Palace and asked for Miss Jasmine Le Valley. It was early for the evening show, but I might catch her if she hadn't gone out to dinner. I recognized the rasping voice of the dragon who watched the stage door.

"Yeah?"

"This is the *New York Globe,* Sandy Blunt. I'd like to speak to Miss Jasmine Le Valley."

"She went out to eat." The voice jolted at me, and hung up. I looked at the receiver an instant, then hung up.

"That was short!"

Pat Curry grinned and returned to his desk. I puttered around for a few minutes, and ambled back into the dead files library, the place where Johnnie and I had, almost three weeks ago now, found out about the ugly tragedy that had marked the beginning of the fateful story of Michael Rawn.

I had taken a paper down trying to get my mind off the haunting

95

fear that seemed to envelop me more closely with every day that passed, when a copy boy bawled my name the length of the office.

"Yes, what is it?"

"Phone for Blunt."

I went forward and took it.

"Sandy? This is Johnnie. I'm down at the Rose Palace. I went down to get a look at that Jasmine Le Valley you talk about . . . well . . . they just came on the stage with an announcement that she won't be able to play tonight's shows because of an indisposition.'

My grip tightened on the receiver. "Where are you now?"

"I'm backstage," Johnnie said in a lower voice, "I got in by saying I was a newspaperman."

"Wait there. Find out as much as you can. Where is Le Valley; did you find out?"

"You better come down," John advised, "I think this old boy backstage is getting me all figured out. I'll wait at the stage door."

He hung up, and without a word to the surprised Pat Curry, I grabbed my topcoat and sailed into the elevator. It was no time at all across 42nd Street. It was nothing, perhaps, that Jasmine Le Valley should not feel disposed to perform some evenings but at the same time I was too much on edge to regard lightly any particular out of the regular order that might happen to any of the people in the mystery of Michael Rawn. I couldn't get out of my mind the fact that Jasmine Le Valley might possibly be the one person who could tell me what the vanished letters contained. I ran quickly around to the stage door of the Rose Palace and encountered Johnnie, standing just outside the door waiting for me. I nodded, indicating the inside, and we went in.

"Just a min—ute . . ." The ancient chairman of the backstage intoned. I whipped out my press card, using it with much the same authority that a magician uses a wand.

"Press to see Miss Le Valley," I approached him as I spoke. "Did the management say Miss Le Valley was indisposed? I was to have met her here after the show," I lied. "Where is the manager?"

The old man shook his head, but his tone was easier. "It won't do you no good to stew yourself up," he declared, "and the manager has gone home. It ain't nothing to him; he'll just dock her salary."

I leaned confidentially toward him, a ten-dollar bill between my fingers. "I'm an old friend of Miss Le Valley's," I muttered, "and I'd like to know where she is . . ." His face was as straight as my own as he took the money.

"Now, young man," he drawled, "I honestly don't know for sure. It's this way. Miss Le Valley got a phone call right after she came off stage after the last afternoon show. She seemed excited; said she was going to meet a friend for dinner; that she'd be back for the show."

"What friend? Did she say?"

"No, she didn't say what friend; but she did say it was an *old* friend, I recall that. She didn't say where they was going to eat, but she said it was grand, so I don't suppose you'd find her at the Bar-Grill down the street, where she sometimes went."

"Go on."

He spread his hands. "That's all! She went out to eat at some grand place with this old friend, and just didn't show up for the evening shows. The management docks her, she comes in tomorrow, and because Jazzy's a regular and a pretty good guy, they won't say anything to her. It's the first time she's missed a performance."

Johnnie and I turned away. I was troubled. We walked slowly west on 42nd Street toward a neon sign: Bar-Grill, it flashed in red, then blue. We went in and ordered whiskey straights.

"What do you think?" I asked Johnnie. He lifted his hands in a helpless gesture.

"Well, it often happens, and it's just too normal for words, and it's none of our damn business . . ." he faced me, his lips tightening. "But I would raise a little hell if I were you. It won't cost anything; you could phone . . . hell . . . I don't know what to do . . ."

"I phoned Pat Curry from the theater," I told Johnnie.

"Oh! What did he say?"

My grin twisted miserably. "He said it was a new lead, *if* anything happened to *her.*" I faced Johnnie. "And so far as Mike's concerned, the police wouldn't even care any more. They've been beating around all over the lot about Floyd Harvey; they're concentrating on him. And why should they take my word if they've got Cassidy convinced down at Headquarters?"

We sat there until almost eleven o'clock. I phoned Cassidy. He accepted my news stolidly, and from time to time Johnnie Olds and I would run over to the stage door to find out if Jasmine Le Valley had returned.

She didn't return, and the Rose Palace closed shortly after midnight. I left Johnnie at the subway, and went over to the office.

Staring me in the face like an enormous, masked ghost was the most striking fact of Michael's disappearance—the accumulation of seemingly unrelated incidents—the mixture of events that had remained so unconnected. Added to this overpowering enigma were the people who seemed to me to be passionately interested in those old letters. Lisa, who had stolen them; her father, Sam Cushman, who had possessed them for so short a time; old Mrs. Martin, once their guardian; Jasmine Le Valley, who might know what was in them—and last but not least, the thief who had stolen them from Cushman, and who had them now. And one other fact confronted me with a smile of cruel scorn.

It was the unmitigated cleverness of the criminal Floyd Harvey. In a town where the newspapers, the very population, and the police themselves had spread a close drag-net, Floyd Harvey had walked coolly through every trap; killing, moving, even buying railroad tickets for himself as well as for the target for one of the greatest searches New York had ever seen—Michael Rawn. It was incredible, and its daring, bloodcurdingly menacing.

I sat before my typewriter helplessly, not able to write one word. Finally Pat Curry looked up.

"Why the hell don't you stop mooning around, Blunt; and go on that vacation?"

I disregarded his injunction. "If you were I, just who would you blame? Now generally—just who would you blame? Forget Floyd Harvey. If you had . . ."

Pat Curry put his head on one side. "Hell, I know what you mean! Who would I blame if I had just come into this thing?"

"Yes. Just at a glance, without knowing too much; without knowing what I know, who would you arrest—or go after?"

He smiled. "I'd arrest a guy called Sandy Blunt."

I stood looking at him like a fool. I think my jaw dropped and my mouth came open a little. I know I was quiet for a long time.

"Tell you why . . ." Pat Curry lifted his glasses to the desk and for the first time I saw his eyes. They were dark grey pebbles. I was surprised; I couldn't tell why. He eyed me a minute then went on. "The reason I'd blame you is simple. You're the only one who *really* knows everything about Michael Rawn. You're the only one who has been following the thing through every tiny lead in the case. *Sandy Blunt* is the *only* person who has, from the very first, been *absolutely certain* of the facts. In other words, you could tell *just what you wanted to tell—but you know everything!*" He sat there smiling at me.

I didn't smile. I went back to my typewriter. Pat Curry returned to his work. He had given me quite a jolt. Somehow I felt he was trying to tell me something more than the words he had said. And I knew he would say no more; he meant me to make the most of it.

I was still puzzling them out when the phone rang. It was Cassidy.

"Sandy, me lad, get your coat on. A cop on the beat, way over 42nd Street, near the river, found this Jasmine Le Valley, shot dead."

There had been a feeble attempt to make it look like a burglary. Her purse had been hastily emptied, but they had found her name engraved on an identification bracelet on her ankle. One bullet, shot at close range from the side had entered above one ear and lodged in the brain. Jasmine Le Valley had died before she knew what struck her.

There was nothing more to know. Cassidy promised me details when the ballistics experts got to work. I wanted to know about that bullet. As I watched the meagre crowd, ghostly in the three A. M. river-fog, a terrible depression swept over me. It seemed as though this terror must go on into eternity. Drag-net or not, the killer had returned again. I felt a resurgence of some unnamed fear; almost as though the killer were among us, watching, laughing, waiting. I turned abruptly, deciding I had had enough. Maybe I would take that vacation after all. I felt I was getting more than a full dose.

As I left the quiet, huddled group of policemen, a *Globe* photographer came up to me.

"Blunt, Curry sent me down. You've had a phone call at the office. Johnnie Olds wants you to call him right away. Says it's important."

"Thanks, Sam."

I stepped into the all-night drug store at Times Square and dialed the apartment. Johnnie must have been sitting beside the phone.

"Sandy!" His voice was dully emphatic.

"Yes . . . what is it?"

"Where are you, Sandy?"

"At Times Square. A drug store. Why?"

"I want to meet you right away."

"But, Johnnie, I've got this . . ."

Johnnie's voice rose stridently. "Sandy, I don't care what you've got to do! This is important."

"What is it now?" I questioned listlessly.

"I've got to meet you right now, Sandy. We've got to go to Staten Island. Sandy, it's the Richmond County Hospital. They've found the body of Michael Rawn."

CHAPTER FIFTEEN

It was half-past four when we got to Staten Island. We took a half-hour bus ride and arrived at the Richmond County Hospital, and were directed to the morgue.

As we went down the tiled halls I felt almost another person, a thousand light-years of living away from the Sandy Blunt I had been on that misty-hot Wednesday that was now so dimly gone, yet so terribly vivid. Like a sleep-walker I followed Johnnie and the attendant into the viewing room, with its little ice-box doors in rows on two walls. Through a high window I saw a shimmering star. The attendant stepped to one of the small doors, opened it, pulled out a tray on rollers, and flung back a canvas sheet. I felt the blood drain from my face.

It was my friend—Michael Rawn. It *was* Mike. Through my numbed senses I could feel knowledge creeping like alcohol in the stomach; bringing me alive, making me recognize, making me know. But it was horrible to think that this had been my friend.

The head and hands had been beaten beyond recognition. A dark purple welt crossed the chest. The body was swollen and bluish, yet somehow pinched and small. After a long minute I nodded; the attendant held for my inspection a small bundle of clothes. They were Mike's; I knew them. The attendant spoke in a low voice; I shook myself mentally, listening carefully. The body had been a "floater." It had been in the water for some time, perhaps a week or more. The items of clothing were listed: trousers, white shirt, wallet, keys, vest, topcoat. I motioned that I was satisfied; I could identify the body as that of Michael Rawn. Johnnie spoke to me but I scarcely heard him. Dimly I heard him arrange with the attendant for the funeral. It could be held in the chapel of the morgue. Dully, I agreed. I didn't care. This was the end I had not believed in; the thing I had hoped to avert. I looked at Mike's body again. There was a bluish-purple welt across the instep of both feet. My eyes went to the welt on the chest. Mike had been tortured. I felt slowly rising within me a new kind of determination. I would get this killer if I died for it. A cold resolve sharpened my perceptions, like a sword thrust into my mind. I was no longer frightened nor impressed by this wanton killer. Standing there beside the body of my murdered friend, I could have killed Floyd Harvey without any hesitation. I felt Johnnie touch my arm; we moved to leave.

At the door we met Dan Cassidy and one of his assistants. His face was stolid but sympathetic.

"Sorry, Sandy. It's Mike, all right?"

I nodded, but found myself looking at him directly. I would need everything from now on. I had set my course.

"Find anything out about Le Valley's death, Cassidy?"

"Yes," he replied, "the bullet came from a 32 automatic—same gun as killed Joyce Bennet. No eye-witnesses at all. But from the time the body had been lying there, Sumstein figures she went there to meet someone, and was killed just after dark. But we haven't found anything else."

I made myself go back with him when he went to look at Mike's body. Even Cassidy's unimaginative mind winced before the sight of that mangled, tortured corpse. As he turned away to look at the clothes, Dan Cassidy caught my eye. He shook his head slowly.

"Somebody hated that boy, all right." He was still shaking his head dolefully as he made notes of the articles of clothing.

Johnnie and I left him standing there. We went to the chapel to arrange with the attendant there for a burial. Johnnie talked to me in a low voice of the things we would need to do. Get in touch with Biglow, phone Lady Matilda Wintarthur, buy a plot—somehow it didn't connect with my mind very well. I had my senses hard ahead, straining toward the next issue that Mike's death had brought me. I had to get Mike's killer. With a sudden shock I realized that I could have no peace of mind in this world until I did. Only then would I be able to close the Story of Michael Rawn. I nodded to Johnnie, and he did the arranging with the quiet man in the chapel. At last Johnnie turned to me.

"All right, Sandy, we can go now. We've . . . done all we can."

We returned along the tile hall, and I took one backward glance at the ice-box room slightly behind us. . A large, stout figure in a very well-cut dark suit had entered the room, a handsome derby hat in his hand, coat over his arm. I halted. The figure was familiar. I waited, and Johnnie turned to me frowning. Then I knew. *It was the man who had occupied the box alone, the night Michael Rawn's play had opened!*

I strode to the door of the room where Mike's body lay, and thrust open the door. The attendant turned, and from under the hard light of the hanging lamp I saw again the acquiline nose, the narrow lips, the strong though fleshy jaw of the man who had sat alone. He was looking down at the body on the rolled-out tray. I strode over to the tray, my eyes on this stranger. How had he known so soon that Michael Rawn's body had been found? As I approached, the thin, sinister lips curved up in a smile. His character did not diminish upon inspection. I have never seen, and never expect to see again, so shrewd a face.

"Ah, yes, Mr. Blunt," the man said, as though we were in his living room, "I had hoped to find you here."

"Did you?" I demanded. "Why?"

He hesitated and smiled again, then raised his brows slightly, as though I were hardly in good form. "I hoped you would be here because it seemed inevitable that you and I should meet."

I felt wary and revolted at his presumption; at his coldness and easy sociability. We were talking across the body of Michael Rawn as though it were a tea-table.

"Who are you?" I demanded flatly. His smile deepened, as though he enjoyed my aggravation.

"I am Mr. Valerian," the man said quietly, and added smoothly, "I have just returned from out of town."

"I'm glad to meet you at last, Mr. Valerian, particularly since you phoned me twice some time ago. What can I help you with?"

His smile was quiet, yet it conveyed the feeling that behind his features his mind was working at some problem like a buzz-saw, tearing, shredding. He turned his cold eyes on me.

"Nothing, now." His glance touched the body lying between us.

In the pause that lengthened uncomfortably, I asked suddenly: "How long did you know Michael Rawn, Mr. Valerian?"

He raised his eyes to me, and again that silky smile crossed his thin lips. "I have known Michael for a very long time," he returned firmly. "I knew Michael long before he came to New York; before he went to Westminster College with you, Mr. Blunt."

I was surprised at the knowledge he had revealed. But my anger still welled up inside me, and I felt myself redden as I blurted, "Do you happen to know the details of his disappearance, Mr. Valerian?"

His chuckle was low, pitiless. "Indeed not, Mr. Blunt. I know no more than you do yourself." His frigid eyes sought mine once again; with a strange sense of discomfort I recalled Pat Curry's words concerning the man he would choose for the guilty party.

My dissatisfaction coupled with my shock over this finality lying bruised and horribly dead on the slab before me made me thoughtlessly rude.

"Now you're satisfied, Mr. Valerian? You won't feel the need of phoning me, then being out of town to my calls?"

His voice poured over me like thick cream. He never for a second lost that calm, nor did his eyes grow a shade warmer than they had been when he greeted me.

"On the contrary, Mr. Blunt. I would be most flattered if you could see fit to accept my hospitality, let us say tomorrow afternoon?"

"What for?" I felt crude and I knew I sounded so.

"I have invited Miss Lisa Cushman," he went on imperturbably, ignoring my tone, "and she has been good enough to accept. I felt that perhaps . . ." His voice dwindled, and his eyes held mine shrewdly.

I smiled, twistedly. "Thank you very much, Mr. Valerian, I should be delighted to be your guest."

I could not know what his game was, or even if he had one, but I was not going to miss any opportunity to learn anything I might about Mike. I didn't like the idea of Lisa going to see this man alone. Mr. Valerian moved from the tray that held the body of Mike Rawn, and studied the assortment of clothes the attendant had put off to one side. I noticed that Johnnie had disappeared, and I was starting to the door when Mr. Valerian, Mike's wallet in his hand, spoke to me.

"Could I drop you in town, Mr. Blunt?"

"Thank you, Mr. Valerian; I'd be delighted if you would." I was not going to let him out-smooth me in the least. "I'll locate my roommate and we'll be right with you.".

He chuckled, lifting Mike's trousers in one hand.

"Ah, yes; Mr. John Olds, the painter. A very unique talent; most unique indeed." The flinty grey eyes caught mine once more. "His talent is worth watching." I took a step and he raised his almost oriental brows and went on, "As a painter, I may safely say it." And he chuckled enigmatically.

With a frown I went into the white tile hall to hunt for Johnnie. This Valerian, whoever he was, seemed to know pretty much of everything. I wondered if he had taken the letters. For a large man, he seemed very light and graceful on his feet. He made far less noise walking over the hard floors than I did myself.

I couldn't find Johnnie, and finally the all-night attendant told me that my friend had left, after completing arrangements for the funeral. I nodded my thanks and returned to Mr. Valerian, who was just coming out of the viewing room.

"Mr. Olds has gone?" he anticipated me.

"Yes."

"Well, my car is just outside . . ." We walked through the hall to the driveway. And I got a severe shock.

The car in the driveway was a large black limousine—the car that had followed me twice in the two days after Michael Rawn had disappeared. Sitting in the back of the car, waiting, was Lisa Cushman.

My hello to her was perfunctory. The three of us hardly spoke as the car crossed the bay on the ferry, but once in Manhattan, Mr. Valerian spoke as though we had all been old, dear friends.

"A most harrowing experience, Miss Cushman," he affirmed, as though continuing a conversation. "You were right not to go in."

After a pause, Lisa asked, "It was . . . it was he, then?"

"Yes; it was Mike's body," I blurted.

We turned off the Express Highway at 72nd Street, and went north on West End Avenue. As I got out of the car, Lisa, with a slight smile, took my hand.

"I'll call for you tomorrow, for a change," she said softly. "I want you to go to Mr. Valerian's with me."

I gave him a half-belligerent look.

"Certainly."

Mr. Valerian reached out his hand, and his smile seemed benevolent. "Mr. Blunt, I shall be honored to receive you tomorrow. I confess I must have your advice on a most important matter. I had thought to be able to work out my own salvation, but I fear I am not sufficient."

Mystified, I watched the big car move off toward Riverside Drive through the coming dawn. As I opened the front door to the hall, I wondered how Mr. Valerian, who seemed to have such an accurate knowledge of my affairs, could need my help. I was pondering the meaning of the invitation to his place as I went up the three flights to the apartment.

I had got to the foot of the stairs to the third floor, when I heard a quick step behind me. I started to turn, a sudden thrill of warning plucking my nerves. Almost before I could move, something cracked down on my head; a shower of red stars flared up before my eyes. I struggled to stay on my feet, to turn and confront my assailant.

Fighting with all my will to stay erect, I felt my knees buckle and knew I was sinking down . . . down into blackness . . . at the mercy of that footstep, that shadow . . . the killer of . . . I' swooped on and down into complete, motionless oblivion.

Vast ages later I came to, to find someone holding my head, and talking to someone who also knelt beside me. It was Johnnie and he was talking to two of the neighbors who had come out onto the hall landing, evidently hearing the commotion.

"He'll be all right now," Johnnie was saying, "I can get him up the stairs. . ." I moaned, and Johnnie looked down at me; his face moving eerily to my eyes. I had a throbbing ache at the back of my skull. "Are you all right, Sandy?"

I nodded feebly, and slowly Johnnie helped me to my feet. The neighbors, assured again that Johnnie could manage me, left. I took hold of the railing and with the other arm about Johnnie's shoulders, navigated the last flight of stairs.

"I heard something fall," Johnnie informed me, "and then someone running down the stairs. I was expecting you, and looked out. You were lying at the foot of the stairs just below me, moaning. I must have scared . . . scared him away."

I said nothing. My head ached worse than ever, now that I moved. Johnnie got me to bed. As I put my head down on the pillow, a thousand sparks burst in my head again. I groaned and turned on my side. Johnnie smiled tiredly as he turned out the light.

"You'll be all right? Want me to call a doctor?"

"Don't call anyone for three weeks." I mumbled, "I just want to lie here and sleep."

Johnnie smiled wanly and the room dropped into darkness.

For a long time, it seemed, I lay there, wanting to sleep but unable to keep the thudding pain from sweeping over me in needling waves. At last I fell into a restless stupor, dim and swirling. I ran from something, running and running, and finally, around a corner that I knew was safe, I paused, breathless; and turned, shrinking with fear to find the jungle cat—*that animal*—staring at me, gleefully, its heavy breath triumphant and evil. I sat bolt upright in bed, my head booming like an aboriginal tom-tom. As my breathing quieted, I could hear Johnnie snoring. I got my flashlight from under my pillow and groped my way to the bureau, into Johnnie's drawer at the very bottom, where we kept our bottle of Old Forrester. I wanted the biggest drink in the world; it would knock me out and I would sleep, dead to the world and the pain that seemed to reach into every artery and vein in my body. I fumbled quietly through Johnnie's sweaters and socks, keeping my light off so as not to wake him. My hand touched something cold, and I lowered my hand to grip the bottle. Suddenly my pain was forgotten. A cold sweat broke out all over me. My hand was gripping a gun!

I put on my flashlight and looked, carefully, into the drawer. The gun was a 32-caliber automatic. Beside it was a small envelope with a number scrawled in pencil. The number said 88th St. With trembling fingers I tore the envelope open. There was a key, a key to a Yale lock. I held my breath, my heart thudding like a well-driller.

In the silence of the inky room I could hear Johnnie's easy, regular snoring.

CHAPTER SIXTEEN

Michael Rawn was buried in Rosemont Cemetery, within walking distance of the Richmond County Morgue. It was a raw, dismal day, with grey skies veiled with skidding, ragged clouds, which dropped rain intermittently all morning. Only Lisa, Johnnie, I and, surprisingly, Mr. Valerian, attended Michael's body to the grave. None of us spoke at all, and as the first shovel of wet yellow earth hit the wooden box with its final thud, I glanced at the suave Valerian. His face was preoccupied and thoughtful, as though he were carefully assembling the pieces of a mosaic. Lisa was dry-eyed and seemed shrunken and tiny to my eyes. Johnnie was quiet and wide-eyed, and I studied him as we stood across the pitiful lonely grave of our friend.

I could not forget my discovery of the night before. My mind, hardened by the two attempts on my life as well as by the irrevocable fact of Michael's burial, had sharpened my thinking; hardened it to the point where I now regarded anyone, whatever his connection with me or with Mike himself, as a suspect. It had come to me in a flash during my sleepless night after the discovery of the gun, that there was only one person in the world who knew as much of Michael Rawn as I did; one person who had from the first known everything I knew, who had been in complete touch with every fact of the case. That person was John Olds.

Mr. Valerian had taken Lisa's arm to help her back to his car, in which we all had come. Johnnie was following them down the slight slope over the curled, wet grass. I stood a dull moment, watching the undertaker's assistant putting the scant flowers on the dismal, lumpy, mound of clay. Lisa had sent red roses, Johnnie and I had sent roses and white carnations, and Mr. Valerian a huge basket of mixed blooms. I recognized them all as having been around the casket in the chapel.

As I stood there the formally dressed assistant took from the hearse a fourth sheaf of flowers; a magnificent array of jonquils, blue iris, black-eyed susans, daisies, gladiolas. Amazingly attached to the long stems were a number of large, vari-colored orchids!

"May I see the card?" I asked the assistant.

He looked up at me with a professionally sad smile. "I'm sorry, sir, but there was no card. They came in just as we were leaving the chapel. I believe the sender wishes to be anonymous. I could find the name of the florist for you."

"Never mind." I thought of Lady Matilda Wintarthur, who even now must wish to remain nameless in everything that connected her with the name of Michael Rawn, even his funeral. At the car, Lisa and Johnnie and Valerian had turned and were looking at me. I went over to them and told them of the cardless flowers. Lisa smiled wanly, and we got into the car to drive back to Manhattan. As we curved around the drive, I looked back. Michael Rawn was gone. There was only one thing I could ever do for him now. I could get his murderer.

We were silent with our thoughts as the big car hummed north on the express highway, and no one spoke until the car stopped to let me off before the Globe Building. Then Mr. Valerian, his voice amazingly gentle and kind, leaned toward me as I stood on the curb.

"I hope, Mr. Blunt, that this unfortunate business has not upset you too much," he intoned. "I will send my car to pick up you and Miss Cushman early this afternoon."

I smiled grimly. "I'd be glad to come, even after this, Mr. Valerian. Thank you. I'll be ready."

"I'm glad," his chuckle came for the first time that morning, "I'm very glad. You are the man I took you for, Mr. Blunt."

I stared after him, pondering the strange statement, as the car went across 42nd Street, on the way to drop Johnnie at the apartment. We both had been given the day, but I wanted to talk to Pat Curry. He was in his office, and when I came in he looked up as though he had been expecting me.

"Well, Sandy, all over?"

107

I nodded wordlessly. "Yes. I'd like to talk to you."

"Fire away."

"I have a suspicion that I know where I can find Michael Rawn's killer," I said blandly. "If I can bring him in, would you give me a raise?"

"Hell, boy, I'll give you the whole outfit!"

"And a vacation?"

"Listen, Sandy, take a week anyhow! You don't have to bargain with me; you know how I feel about this thing. You've had a helluva time. I tell you, bring in this killer, write me a story on it—and you can write your own ticket." He looked up at me, taking off his glasses, and again I was amazed at the bland coldness of his eyes. "Oh, yes," Curry reminded himself. "Cassidy phoned. He said that when you got in touch with him this morning about that gun and the key that you said were hidden in your apartment—well, anyhow, while you and Olds were at the funeral, he sent a man to your place. The gun is the one that killed Joyce Bennet and Jasmine Le Valley, all right. And the key is the one that fits the room in that 88th Street rooming house. The only finger prints on them were yours, though—probably from handling them last night. No others. Is that what you wanted to know?"

"It is."

There was a pause, then Pat Curry looked up at me quizzically. "You got someone on the hook?"

I nodded, tight-lipped. "The only person who knew everything. The only person it could possibly be."

After another silence, Curry said softly, "John Olds?"

I just looked at him and smiled. "I said I'd get the killer, and I mean it. I'll answer your question when I can bring him in. Then I can write my own ticket, is that right?"

He nodded his head. "The vacation is good this minute. I think you need a week's rest, Blunt."

My lips twisted. "I'm going to get this exclusive. I'm going to get to the bottom of this thing before Cassidy does. It's the only thing left that I can do."

He shook his head. "Go to it."

Without another word I turned and went out. I walked the whole way home, busy with my thoughts. I remembered that John Olds had seemed to make a bee-line for Joyce Bennet at Michael Rawn's party. I wondered what he knew about her, wondered at his faultless performance at Mike's funeral. No slight note had broken our friendship that morning. Johnnie's attitude was a duplicate of mine—two friends burying a third. I thought grimly of what John had said that night when he had been getting ready for Mike's premiere, his statement that Mike had done some very handsome acting while living with us. Well, if I were right, Johnnie had done some pretty fine acting himself. There could be no mistake about the gun and that key. They had been put there by the person who had used them. Somehow I knew I was getting very close to the end. Soon, with careful steps, I must come face to face with the brutal criminal who was the solution to the kidnapping of Michael Rawn.

Going up the three flights of stairs I stepped very easily. As I passed the landing at the end of the second floor hall, I looked around me. I saw that just as the steps started toward the third floor and the apartment where I lived, the doors of the second floor front were set into a small vestibule, hidden from the light that burned in the hall.

In this vestibule my assailant had waited. I had been in luck. My fall had aroused the house, and doors had opened. My would-be killer had fled. Or perhaps he had simply cached his bludgeon in some dark corner to retrieve later, and knelt at my head, coolly pretending that his presence had saved my life! I could feel my jaw work as I thought of it. Now all I had to do was to trap the one person I suspected.

John was not at home and a scrawled note informed me that he had gone to his studio in the Village to paint. I smiled cruelly. It took the hardened soul of a deliberate, calculating intellect to go from a funeral to a paint-box. I locked the door and lay down. I needed a rest, for I had lain sleepless the night before, listening to John Olds' regular low breathing. I wondered now if he had been lying awake, simulating sleep, waiting for my regular breathing to tell him he was safe to try again. I thought myself into a cold rage, and at last rose with a sudden inspiration and went down one flight of stairs to the place where I had been struck. I looked at the doors in the vestibule that gave on the front second floor rooms. One door was locked, but when I tried the one farthest from the hall, the door yielded to my touch.

It was a small single room, and it was empty. Behind the door was a short, round implement, like a truncated baseball bat without the tapered handle. I stood looking at it, then lifted it in my hand. It was a formidable weapon; and I knew now what had been used to club me.

I heard someone coming up the stairs, and I quietly closed the door and stepped into the hall. A man in a chauffeur's uniform inquired, "Mr. Blunt's apartment?"

"I'm Mr. Blunt."

"Mr. Valerian's compliments, Mr. Blunt. He took the liberty to send the car early, since he would like you and Miss Cushman for lunch. Miss Cushman is waiting in the car, Mr. Blunt."

I told him I'd be right down, and as he started back to the street, I ran up to the apartment and washed.

Lisa smiled wanly at me, searching my face with her eyes, and as I got in she took my hand and squeezed it. I returned her smile, but I did not look into her eyes. I felt I had failed up to now. With Michael's body, with his funeral, I felt that I had lost my chance at her friendship. She had loved Michael and I had lost him for her. Deep in my heart I had never believed that Cassidy would find Mike, however he might apprehend the murderer. The primary police function is to protect the public from criminals, and the killer, not Michael Rawn, had been Cassidy's objective from the first. I was the man who had boldly set out to find Michael, and I had failed miserably, as completely as a mortal can fail. Michael was dead, and my best efforts, my determined work, could never bring him back. Lisa and I did not speak as the car swooped us up Riverside Drive.

I have never seen a more luxurious apartment than that of Mr. Demos Valerian. Full of my thoughts as I was, the elegance and taste struck me at once. Paintings I knew to be fabulous originals hung in the foyer. As we sat in the deep cushions of the living room divan, I looked about me curiously. The Oriental servant who had admitted us had left us in the living room while he went to inform Mr. Valerian we had arrived, and my inquiring glance discovered that the whole tone of the room was itself somewhat Oriental. Silk paintings hung on the walls; the furniture had the square corners that are modern, yet they, too, had something of the East about them. The chairs were low, wide rather than high, and the groups of flower arrangements were studied in their grace. The carpet was rich with color, deep, and I knew, priceless. Obviously, Mr. Valerian was a man of great means. One particular thing struck me. The sofa on which Lisa and I sat was on the longest wall in the room, and while the other walls were complete in their decoration, the wall over the sofa was absolutely bare. It was noticeable even in the elegant simplicity through which not one false note rang.

Mr. Valerian came into the room, his weight carried lightly, his steps on the carpet almost soundless as he approached us. "How do you do? I am honored. I have a great deal I would like to discuss, and while this must be a difficult time for both of you, I trust you will bear with me." His brows went up slightly and Mr. Valerian turned to me. "I am particularly interested in your plans for the immediate future, Mr. Blunt. You see, I am intimately concerned with our friend, Michael Rawn."

"I know you are, Mr. Valerian," said Lisa surprisingly, taking my hand. "Sandy will be glad to talk anything over with you." I felt hardly so open as all that, but it was no time to discuss principles.

Mr. Valerian led us to an alcove, and we began one of the best lunches I have ever eaten. Mr. Valerian, to put us at our ease, went on talking as soon as we were seated.

"As I told you, Mr. Blunt, I have known Michael Rawn for a long time. A most remarkable young man. One of my friends in the police department told me of your determination to bring the criminal to justice. A most laudable ambition." His hard, pale eyes held mine. "Frankly, how do you feel your progress has been, as to result?"

I grinned tightly. "Frankly, Mr. Valerian, I feel like a complete bust! A wash-out!"

He smiled, and that smooth chuckle rose from him like a hidden, bubbling spring. "A hard summary for a young man. Hard, indeed, Mr. Blunt. But you must not blame yourself. The case of Michael Rawn has undermined the confidence of the police throughout the whole country, I assure you. What is your next step, if I may ask?"

I looked at him steadily. "I'm going to get Mike's killer."

He laughed his deep laugh once more. "Excellent! I like to see a man who can stay at a thing." There was a short pause, then his voice dropped, and his mouth became a cruel beak. "Mr. Blunt, I am your admirer. I have something to tell you; something that may surprise you."

I glanced at Lisa; she was busy with her soup. I met the calculating eyes of Mr. Valerian. Suddenly I wondered just who he was, and what. What nationality could produce that hawk-like face, those cruel eyes and mouth, that gentle, yet chilly voice?

"The first time I met Michael Rawn in New York," Mr. Valerian said, "I knew at once I was meeting an extraordinary human being. He was completely equipped for success. For Michael Rawn, success

111

was as inevitable as death is to all of us. He was a fabulous young man." Mr. Valerian broke into his frigid rumble of laughter. "And Michael Rawn knew he was gifted; no one knew it better. It gave him a determination that was invincible."

"You must have known Mike well," I commented.

"Indeed I did," Valerian acceded, "I helped Michael Rawn; I was glad to assist him. Which brings me to my point. I had loaned him quite a lot of money, Mr. Blunt. When Michael disappeared I had a definite reason for my interest. I, too, want the criminal who killed Michael Rawn, and made off with a vast sum of my money!"

"I see," I remarked somewhat bitterly. Mr. Valerian caught my eye and continued.

"But my interest was not so much in the money as in finding Michael Rawn himself. Michael interested me. He interests me still. To be brief, Mr. Blunt, I would like to assist you in any way in whatever course you decide to follow."

I looked at him directly. "Just how could you help, Mr. Valerian?"

"I think I could give you a valuable piece of information, Mr. Blunt," his voice was very low, his tone smooth as velvet.

"Yes?"

"Yes," Valerian smiled. "You see, I think Michael Rawn is still alive."

"*Alive!*" I almost shouted, "why, just this morning . . ."

My eyes must have looked like doorknobs, because Mr. Valerian gave his rumbling laugh. "Yes, I believe that Michael is now alive; held, perhaps, in some unlikely place. . ."

"What makes you say this?" I inquired sharply, then shook my head. "It's all wrong—I saw him . . . with my own eyes!"

"Because I have reason to believe that the killer still has a use for Michael Rawn."

"What use? The killer has Michael's money. This is insane!" I rose. "If this is what you brought me . . ."

"Please hear me out," he persuaded, and I grudgingly resumed my chair. "That is what I do not know," Valerian admitted smoothly, "and that is why I asked you here. I myself have tried to find Michael. You have tried, and the estimable police have tried. The killer has eluded us all. But if we were to join forces, perhaps we might do better."

I smiled grimly at the thought. It was nearly a month since Michael had disappeared. I firmly believed him dead. But I was in no position to dictate ideas. I had failed. Valerian might be right. If we joined forces . . .

"What do you want of me; have you some idea?"

He was quiet for a minute, and Lisa looked up at him. The look of eagerness I saw there made me turn my eyes to Valerian's face. He was considering some plan, and his shrewd eyes never left mine.

At last he said, "You began your search for Michael with the most difficult handicap in existence, Mr. Blunt. That is your friendship for Michael. You knew things that colored your thoughts without your realizing it. My plan is this: pare your intellect down to bare intuition. Think! If you knew Michael well, wanted to hide him forever, let us say, where would you take him?"

"I'd murder anyone I had to hide forever," I determined, going full circle in my thoughts.

"Let us say you did not need to watch your captive; that within his bondage he had certain small freedom, yet he could never run away?"

I laughed. "It's impossible."

"Allow me my fancy, Mr. Blunt. Without consideration of your friend, where would you hide him?"

"You knew Michael," I parried. "Where would you hide him?"

Valerian grew suddenly stern. "I was not perpetrating a poor joke, Mr. Blunt," he declared, "I am in grim earnest. I have reason to believe that my scheme is the only way the killer can be found, by finding where he has hidden Michael Rawn. I knew Michael after he had come to New York. I do not know where he might well be kept without his trying to escape. That is something only you can tell me, Mr. Blunt. What place would Michael Rawn be content to remain a captive? Ask yourself that question."

There was a grim silence, then he went on, his voice cold but persuasive. "Mr. Blunt, I have here an envelope. If you will do this for me—assist me in finding Michael Rawn—the envelope is yours. It contains ten thousand dollars."

"What is your stake in finding Michael, assuming he *is* alive?"

Mr. Valerian indicated his luxurious apartment with a wave of his hand. "I did not have to labor, to face the world with work and talent to have all this, Mr. Blunt. I inherited wealth. I might very well of necessity have become a great artist had I been poor. Michael was the type of person who makes an immortal impression on the world. I am interested in that impression. I am laboring to bring Michael back to his world."

I thought for a moment; the letters out of the long ago— Michael's long struggle—I looked up to meet Valerian's eyes. I nodded. As I did so a strange light shone in his face, made it for a moment a mask of cunning. I hesitated, but I had committed myself.

"Very good, Mr. Blunt. Take the envelope. Think about our conversation; act on it. By all means, act on it, Mr. Blunt. If you like, tell Miss Cushman what you finally decide to do. But remember, do it soon! Every day . . . ."

I stood. "Mr. Valerian, I can't take any money for an arrangement like this. I want to find Michael. You say he may be alive. I'll take the chance on my own."

He nodded. "As you will, Mr. Blunt, but promise me you will give my idea close consideration?"

I looked at Lisa; her eyes impaled me.

"I will," I promised Valerian, "if you think I can help."

"I know that I cannot find him, the police have failed, and you are the only person who knew the deepest feelings of our friend, Michael Rawn. If he is alive, anywhere, you can sense where he might be. Do not think too much, Mr. Blunt; it is a fault of our modern civilization upon which there is too much emphasis. No intellect has found this killer, Mr. Blunt. Only the most primitive instinct can find him."

I laughed. "Well, Mr. Valerian, I'll give it a try. It'll be good for a news story, no matter how it comes out."

We all laughed, and the meal went to its conclusion with a lighter tone. Mr. Valerian told us of his painting, his inheritance. He was Greek, and his father had left him an importer's fortune. He had come to New York to spend it, to learn of life in the market-place of the world. As we left it was almost evening, and with some surprise I realized that I had had the first good time since that Wednesday Michael had vanished.

At the door I thanked Mr. Valerian, and renewed my promise to hypnotize myself into thinking where Michael was held captive. My brain rejected the idea, but elimination had proved that there was nothing else left. I decided that I would take the vacation Pat Curry had allowed me, and use it to employ the intuition Mr. Valerian believed in so much. It seemed like taking a course in crystal-gazing, but what else was there?

As we left Mr. Valerian took my hand. His face was grim.

"I would advise great care, Mr. Blunt. If you leave the city, inform me or Miss Cushman. Intuition is useless unless employed with all the savagery from which it springs. Remember that. Along with its certainty it foreordains certain danger and death."

CHAPTER SEVENTEEN

That evening I got an advance from Pat Curry, ostensibly for a vacation. I told him I didn't know my plans, which was true enough, but the fact was that I had entered into the spirit as well as the word of Valerian's plan, and I wanted to be absolutely free in case mental lightning happened to strike! I had not thought any more of Johnnie, and less about Floyd Harvey, for whom the police were still carefully searching. Another reporter was assigned to cover Cassidy while I was away, so I left feeling that I had nothing between me and my next idea, whatever it might happen to be.

Valerian had asked me to try pure instinct. All right, I would! In my deepest heart I knew Michael Rawn was dead, but I needed a rest, and now was the best time to take it. I could get back to John Olds or Floyd Harvey later.

I walked aimlessly through Central Park, across from Fifth Avenue to the reservoir, and around and around it until I was tired. I concentrated on Michael Rawn, on the boy I had known so well— better than anyone in the world. I thought of his talent, his ambition, his overpowering ability to work. It was of a piece, all a part of his tremendous capacity for turning out his own type of success. His heart, I felt, must be deep and inscrutable. I thought about what Michael had liked in school, where I had of necessity known him most intimately. His likes were very simple. He could get more pleasure out of a walk than any of us could on the trips to Youngstown to get drunk. He had been quiet to live with. That was something that would never show to the casual observer, for Michael's brilliance showed in his wit and his cleverness, which was shot with the gold of his quick mind, and utterly disguised his natural simplicity.

Thinking of Michael, I came out of the Park at Columbus Circle, took the Seventh Avenue Subway, and rode uptown. I did not get off, just rode and rode, thoughts going through and around my mind— thoughts not of Mike's disappearance, but of Michael himself. I consciously kept thinking of him, his personality, every least thing about him, shutting out firmly all the theories I had built from facts I had learned first-hand or from Curry or from Cassidy. It was a last stand. I tried to face it directly, without the slightest circumvention. The five o'clock crowd rushed on and up and off, and the seven o'clock crowd came down and got off to go to the theater. I rode on, up and down to the eternal clacking of the wheels on the buried rails, through the forests of supporting pillars that upheld the busy subterranean caves.

And nothing occurred to me. If instinct were dangerous, as Valerian had prophesied, then I seemed safe enough. But the more I thought about Michael, the more a longing came over me to see once again, if only for a day or so, the place where we both had been happiest; where I knew that Michael had been most himself. It was childish, the old-grad complex striking at last when I was weakest, but I figured what the hell! I was on a vacation, why ought I not take to the woods? It was a short ride, and I might as well have it.

I got out of the subway at 79th Street. It was late at night. I had forgotten my watch when I washed to go to Valerian's, and I wanted to get it and to pack. The apartment seemed quiet as I went up the three flights, and I watched almost unconsciously the tiny vestibule where I had been struck down. I wondered with a strange detachment what had become of the short, ugly club that had been behind the door in the vacant single room. Somehow I seemed separated from it now, as though it were a part of another life, a life long gone—finished with the funeral of Michael Rawn.

Johnnie was not at home, and after I had packed and strapped on my watch, out of curiosity I went to the bureau and took a drink. The gun and the envelope with the key had gone, spirited away, no doubt, by one of Cassidy's good men and true. Well, John Olds could not get away without considerable comment, and Cassidy had long ago told me that he was having everyone with the remotest connection with the case carefully shadowed. No, John Olds would keep until my return.

It was midnight when I was ready to go. I hesitated about phoning Lisa, but I sat down and dialed her number. Her sleepy voice answered.

"Lisa, this is Sandy."

With an almost audible jolt she came awake. "Where are you going?" she asked clairvoyantly.

"Just away. I won't be gone two days."

"Sandy," she pleaded, "I want you to tell me where you're going. I've got to know, Sandy."

"Now Lisa," I demurred, "It's just a little trip back to my old school. It doesn't mean a thing. I'm tired and want to get away for a time."

Her voice lowered. "All right, Sandy. Just be sure to keep in touch with me—please!" Her tone was so urgent that I promised. "All right, Lisa, I will. I promise." I wanted very much to call her Lisa dear, but didn't quite dare. But I thought it, and the thought stayed with me all the way down on the subway to Penn Station.

It was eight o'clock when I arrived at the Union Station in Pittsburgh, a morning full of the particular grey-wet dark blueness that is Pittsburgh downtown before noon. I walked the two blocks to the Harmony Bus line and bought a ticket for New Wilmington. The bus was not very crowded, and I slept fairly well on the back seat, my long legs stretched out full length at last. By ten I had taken my bag from the roof of the bus and was established in a room at the Tavern, a neat place that had been *the* place to take your girl to dinner in my school days.

As I walked over the campus I could almost feel the aches and tangles of the past weeks leaving me. Even my head, which had begun to boom when I got off the train, stopped its constant throbbing. The air was cold and invigorating, and at last I found myself leaving the narrow confines of the village and striking out manfully on the road that led north to Mercer, the county seat. It was a typical country road for this section of Pennsylvania, hard surfaced, but choosing to wind around the hills rather than to cut through them as the larger highways did. I enjoyed the scenery, and the sense of peaceful quiet that pervaded the area, undisturbed as it had been for fifty years by any sort of "improvement." The farms were small and neat, but there was about them that careless placement of implements that told of everyday living, the constant daily return to an earth that richly welcomed care and labor.

I walked for what I knew to be almost ten miles, and I began to feel acutely the pangs of hunger. At school we had always stopped at one or another of the friendly farmhouses for a glass of warm milk. I decided to bring the picture of my return to the scene to full focus by renewing the custom now.

I knocked at the kitchen door of the next farm, and a pleasant-faced old man opened to me.

"I beg your pardon, sir, but I've been walking a long way . . ."

117

He held the door wide. "Come in. Come in."

I did, and he went directly across the kitchen, and brought a pitcher of milk from the cold-room. "Have a glass of milk, and maybe you could eat a fresh-baked cookie."

I smiled and he sat down to join me.

"Come from far, mister?"

"Just down New Wilmington . . ."

"I see. Live there? Maybe you teach at the college?"

"No," I admitted, "I'm just a visitor."

"Well, seem to be quite a lot this summer," he rejoined. "A lot of 'em. Nice to have, for the trade. 'Course we out here don't see much of 'em. But it's nice to talk to a new tongue now and then."

"This is good milk and wonderful cookies."

"Help yourself, mister. I'm alone here today. Daughter and her husband are in to New Castle, gadding around trying to buy her a new coat or somewhat, don't know exactly. As I say, we see a lot of the visiting folk, being right on the Mercer road this way. Most all gone now. Except it is good for the real estate values, my son-in-law says. Take for instance the old McGarvey place. Bought not a six-months ago; fixed up like all gee-whilikers, and right now you'd never know the place. And Bert, that's my son-in-law, says the value of all our places will go right up in the air, if these out-of-towners gets to buying them for summer places. Of course, now, there's taxes to consider, I told Bert. That's somewhat else again. The place is better, but I says to him, the taxes gets higher and higher until nobody but one of them out-of-towners can afford to live out along this road! It's something to take into mind, I say!"

I rose and thanked him.

"That ain't nothing, mister. Just any time you're out along this way."

I left promising to return. I was rested now and decided to walk further on the road toward Mercer, instead of turning back. The road had always been one of my favorite walks, and every step took me closer to the quiet frame of mind that had been growing like some beautiful magic bloom since I had first left the bus.

I came around a bend in the road, strode with firm step over the crest of a hill, and stopped. A tiny valley dropped below me, and lying in the curve of a small brook was a lovely cottage. It was not a farm house, although at one time it might have been. It was newly renovated, and the picket fence was fresh and straight with new paint and pride. Smoke lifted like a dainty plume from the whitewashed chimney. It had the air of restful retreat. It was not a place to work, it was a place to loaf.

I resolved to pretend I had not already stopped for milk and cookies, and to make my official stop at this beautiful little house. I admired it more and more as I approached. In the rear were two neat compost heaps and a garage. Someone from Pittsburgh who had retired was doing for the rest of his life what I was doing just for these two glorious days. I smiled for the first time, happily; the first time for almost a month. I stepped up and lifted the tidy brass knocker on the blue-painted door. In a moment the door swung open. My heart leaped into my throat.

I was face to face with Floyd Harvey—blue-eyed, cropped, thinner, but Floyd Harvey!

"Harvey . . ." I took a step forward, but the figure in the door smiled almost sadly, and spoke very low. All at once I felt there was something terribly wrong, deadly wrong, about this Floyd Harvey. Then he spoke.

"Sandy. It's not Harvey. Be careful. You're being watched." His voice dropped and now my startled eyes confirmed his words:

"Sandy, this is Michael Rawn . . ."

CHAPTER EIGHTEEN

The living room was rather large, and one of the loveliest I have ever seen. A bright fire burned in the fireplace. The furniture was all chintzes and polished wood, and somehow in November there were bowls of spring flowers, daffodils and narcissus and tiny pots of violets. There was a door at the other end of the room, into the kitchen, I presumed; and unconsciously at the sight of that door my wariness returned. I remembered suddenly that this was a prison—that we might be watched. Michael's disguise had thrown me off momentarily, but I could feel my heart ease at the sound of that deep, cadenced voice. It was never the voice of an understudy.

"All right to talk, Mike?" I whispered uneasily.

He stood with his back to me at the desk near the door at the far end of the room. "It's all right now, Sandy; now that we aren't in the front doorway."

"Mike," I offered quickly, urgently, "I came to get you out of here. What can I do? Are . . . they coming back . . . do we have any time?"

He returned with a large brown legal envelope in his hand; motioned me to sit on the sofa across from him in a big barrel chair.

"Mike; we ought to hurry, shouldn't we?"

For answer he took from the envelope a pack of letters. "These ought to explain," he said softly. I took them, suddenly staring. *They were the letters I had first seen wrapped in the pink ribbon!* My hand trembled as I opened the first one.

After the first three I felt let down. They seemed too simple; not at all what I had expected. And they had nothing to do with Michael. They were more or less the same; maybe a dozen or so of them. Love-letters to the woman who had called herself Jasmine Le Valley, written by her darling Sammy. Very passionate and very ordinary.

"But Mike . . ." I looked up, puzzled. Then my speech froze in my throat. Something was wrong; *his eyes were dark!* His eyes—like a flash I knew—Mike had come to the door wearing blue-colored contact lenses! He had often spoken of getting them if he needed glasses. Watching my face, Mike laughed, deeply. I looked, wide-eyed, and felt sweat start out on my forehead, drop down my ribs from my armpits. I was transfixed with shock and surprise! Suddenly, I knew I ought not to have come. A wave of pure, unreasoning terror crept over me like a rising tide of petrifying coldness. I saw what he had held in his lap, and half rose.

Mike had taken a gun from the folder while I read the letters and was sitting there with his quiet smile, pointing that gun at me—waiting.

I backed away to the edge of the sofa, more in shock than fear. I had a frightful lightning burst of knowledge. I saw the portrait, Michael holding the world . . . he could do anything, and he meant to kill me in cold blood! I knew it now; knew Michael Rawn had been waiting for me to come to him. I was the only person in the world who could give him away. Johnnie might, but would never bother. Only I had been friend enough and fool enough to fall into his patient trap. I had written about him and he must get rid of my seeking. He sat there, Michael Rawn, with his hair cut off and bleached, his eyes which had been blue at his convenience. In a tight rage of discovery I heard myself choke out:

"Harvey . . . you killed him . . . *It was Harvey we buried for you!*"

"That's right, Sandy," Michael answered quietly, standing.

Suddenly I was wildly furious, sick at my cosmic ignorance in befriending Michael Rawn, at the unguarded feelings that had betrayed me. With nauseating recognition I knew now why I had instinctively hated the Valerian portrait. Mike's lowered chin, those wide, intent eyes, that quietly working mouth—they were the features of the jungle animal that haunted my dream!

Michael Rawn walked silently toward me, stalking. My thoughts were avalanched by an overwhelming rush of physical fear. I had no chance in this arena of death, tricked out in the form and shape of a country living room. I moved around the end of the sofa, my eyes on his gun, across the fireplace, toward the far end of the room—away from the burning, glowing eyes of the predatory human animal across from me.

Crack!

The gun made a terrific clap; I felt myself lurch sideways. My arm was hot and wet and I knew I had been hit. Michael came a step nearer. I cast around for some weapon. I had to delay that march of death! My only chance was delay—time, precious and going with every breath. I needed time—time to get to that door at the back of the room—away from Michael Rawn.

I dodged as he raised the gun. It went off, then again. One of the small bowls of violets crashed to the hearth, shattering into a thousand splinters. The fire hissed viciously at the blooms and they curled and died. I heard dimly the sound of a passing car, felt with crazy anguish its freedom—the dear freedom I would not know again. My shirt was clinging to me, wet through. Mike raised the gun and shot again. I heard the whistle and a soft plop as the bullet struck the upholstery of the chair I dropped behind. Mike had two more bullets. I retreated almost to the kitchen door, pulling that high-backed, heavily padded chair in my wake. One brief respite and I could throw myself against that door! My eyes glued to that slow, careful figure, intent on my death. I reached out, and grasping the desk chair by one leg, I crashed it against the floor. The frail structure gave way. I held a spindly leg in my hand, my only defense against certain death. Mike looked down one second at his gun. I turned and flung myself against that door—it was my one chance—and my heart dropped sickeningly within me! THE DOOR WAS BOARDED UP!

. I turned, frantic, raised my club with an empty sense of unbearable futility. Mike had raised that gun for a point-blank shot. I gathered myself for one last awful leap. I heard Michael's quiet laughter, throaty, triumphant—there was an ear-shattering explosion and an echo and my last thought was a deep sighing relief at a merciful, endless, relaxed darkness . . . forever and forever . . . and I felt myself falling, sinking, wondering vaguely how I could have feared death that was so deep a freedom . . . so peacefully silent . . . so swiftly ebbing into nothingness . . .

On a dreary, raining day two weeks later I stood with Lisa in the Park Avenue apartment that had been Michael Rawn's, while Mr. Demos Valerian supervised the removal of the furnishings, which he had bought. Lisa's hand was in my good one. I wore the other in a sling, better now but still sore from Michael's bullet. It was the first time we three had been alone together, and we were matching the pieces of the mystery of Michael Rawn.

"It was a close thing, Sandy, my friend," Mr. Valerian said in his smooth voice. "Had Miss Cushman and I not arrived at the front door when we did, Michael certainly would have finished you off in high style." He chuckled appreciatively. "Probably you would be under his fine compost heap right now."

"I've wondered a lot why you aren't being held for manslaughter, Mr. Valerian," I laughed.

"My friend," he smiled, "I am deputized by no one other than your old friend, Inspector Dan Cassidy. I asked him not to mention my name to you; I chose to follow you for some time myself. Mine is the big car that caused you so much annoyance when you began to hunt Michael."

"Yes," I admitted with a sigh, "I guess I wasn't much good as a sleuth; I was so certain Michael was my friend."

"On the contrary, Mr. Blunt," Valerian asserted, "no one but you could have found him; no one but you could have proved what the police found utterly incomprehensible! I tried to discover Michael's hiding-place, as did Miss Cushman. We were helpless until you finally came onto him. Your intuition found him, and Michael feared your search above all other things."

"You've talked to Cassidy and Pat Curry?" I asked. "Just what was Mike's actual scheme?"

"We've put it together out of what we know, plus your own articles," Valerian's shrewd eyes caught mine. "It is, like all good art, remarkably simple. Michael Rawn had set himself to retire to the country. His pattern was suggested to him by Floyd Harvey's red wig! Michael suddenly saw that if Floyd with a wig could look like Michael Rawn, then, with colored contact lenses, and his hair cut short and bleached, *Michael Rawn looked like Floyd Harvey*—with one great advantage! *If Michael possessed the wig he could also represent himself on occasion!* That was the basis of the double deception, which Michael used with telling effect when he bought tickets at Pennsylvania Station.

"Michael's aim was to retire richly to the country; to live a life he loved and he felt had been brutally denied him in childhood. He was a classic paranoid personality, and his abnormality took a strange form. He *enjoyed* appearing absolutely normal, which made him almost impossible to detect! He had enlisted his greatest potential enemies as his friends, a feat which nearly cost you your life three different times, Mr. Blunt!

"But to go on. I loaned Michael a large sum of money to back his show; I was very interested to see what course he would take. He exceeded my wildest imaginings! When he first sought a producer a year before he disappeared, Michael overheard a word dropped by the good Miss McGonigle, and he knew he had found a way to start a fortune. Instead of using my money to back his play, he put it in his checking account; then, acting on Miss McGonigle's innocent hint, Michael struck up an acquaintance with the mother of Miss Jasmine Le Valley. Michael rooted until he found some compromising letters which Miss Le Valley had kept out of sentiment; and over many months Michael finally blackmailed Mr. Cushman into backing his play as well as handing him huge sums of money privately. He knew Mr. Cushman would not risk his public reputation by exposure. All in all, Michael collected over a period of six months or nine a sum of over two hundred thousand dollars. The play itself was never much to Michael but an opening wedge. He did not love anything but his strange, twisted dream of lovely country living, no matter how he got the money.

"The night of October the 27th found Michael ready. He had persuaded Floyd Harvey to take a room on 88th Street by telling him that he was in love with Harvey's wife and would give Harvey money to facilitate the divorce. Michael asked Floyd to meet him in the 88th Street room, and to bring the wig. Floyd must have forgotten it; leaving it in Michael's box at the theater. Michael returned for it the night you nearly caught him in the theater. But the night of the double disappearance, Michael Rawn killed Floyd Harvey, leaving the gruesome stain you found on the floor. Then he dressed the grisly corpse in some of his clothes, and flung him into the Hudson River. The authorities at Richmond Morgue verified that the body had been dead when it was submerged.

"Michael stayed in the 88th Street room, under what disguise we do not know, until he emerged to murder Martha Wain. He feared she knew too many details of the relationship that existed, uneasily enough, among the three of them. It is Inspector Cassidy's belief, and mine, that Floyd had tried in a small way to blackmail Michael. Michael led Martha Wain to believe that he would take her away with him—but when her estranged husband disappeared, she became panic-stricken, at last phoned you, Sandy, and was murdered by Michael at the very minute she tried to help you!

"Michael had bought the house in Mercer County, Pennsylvania, quite some time ago, and his trips between killings were in the way of preparing his house for habitation; an extremely cool plan! But events began to pile up on Michael. He had to return to get the last of his money—his avarice would let him leave nothing behind—and this he did in the guise of Floyd Harvey, to keep the myth alive! It was inevitable that Floyd should be hailed as the killer, and Michael caused him to appear every so often; daringly and ingeniously.

"Poor Miss Joyce Bennet was unfortunate. She died simply because Michael recalled Floyd Harvey's friendship for her, and did not know how much Floyd had told her. Because Michael had presumably been kidnapped, his notes and telegrams or phone calls to his prospective victims, telling them he would call on them, urging them to utmost secrecy—those messages had all the confidence of state secrets! Michael's victims went to their deaths, or invited Michael and his deadly purpose to their own rooms, firm in the belief that they were helping him to escape his captor! Thus he lured Miss Le Valley to her doom on the river bank at 42nd Street, when she began to importune you for the letters in her clumsy phone call! Michael Rawn killed as some people cross the street—to his emotionless, warped intellect he was simply opening the way to a peaceful future!"

"But why would Michael need to bludgeon father for the letters?" Lisa demanded.

"That was an unusually ugly facet of Michael's nature," Mr. Valerian continued. "He was intensely avaricious. He felt that those letters were a certain source of income. He had to come back to New York to get them. He first asked Biglow to keep them, then, with his cruel irony, asked Miss Cushman to give them into her father's keeping—so he would be certain where to find them when he came for them! Mr. Cushman confided in me and I prompted Miss Cushman's theft." Mr. Valerian looked at me sternly. "Michael had further blackmailed Mr. Cushman into assisting him in his suit with Miss Cushman; feeling that once the two of them married, Mr. Cushman would be silent forever. A frightful and clever plan! Miss Cushman read the letters while they were in her hands—her father insisted— and she knew in a flash that Michael could never be dead! Miss Cushman and I consulted, Mr. Blunt; and while we realized that only you could help us, still, because of your firm friendship for Michael Rawn, we could not risk alienating you by telling what we felt to be the truth!"

Lisa interrupted. "I got hold of Mr. Valerian and Pat Curry when you told me you were going to your old school," she said tenderly, "and when Pat told us where that was, Mr. Valerian and I set out in his car. We guessed you wouldn't take a gun!"

I squeezed her to me. "Then the slug of hair I found the first time I came here," I indicated the rooms on the balcony, "was from Mike cutting his hair short? And those mysterious brusnes and the scissors Biglow bought—no wonder I couldn't find them! Michael had taken them to the country!"

"Exactly," Valerian agreed, "and it is my personal belief that we were looking at Michael dressed in Floyd's wig that night the play opened, for Mike had no time to prepare his short, bleached haircut except before the theater! Another reason why he knew he had to murder Floyd was because Floyd must have loaned him that wig on opening night."

"Then the blond hair in Martha Wain's hand as she lay dead was Michael's?" I interpolated, and Mr. Valerian nodded.

"I knew Martha Wain must be dead, and a man on the street confirmed my guess," he declared. "So I followed you that night for the second time. I was gratified that you did not work with the police. A very brave man, Mr. Blunt!"

I smiled in thanks and he proceeded almost dreamily. "It was faultless, the way Michael could cover every eventuality; his battering in the head of Harvey, to prevent dental identification. And the hands, so those who knew him could not compare Floyd Harvey's spatulate digits to his own delicate fingers! Not to mention his adroit planting of the murder gun, with which he had killed the Misses Bennet and

Le Valley, in the bureau of worthy Mr. Olds, along with the tell-tale key to the room on 88th Street!"

"Of course; Mike had kept his old key to your apartment! He'd gone there before Johnnie and I got back from the Richmond Morgue!" Light dawned on my mind with sudden clarity. "But how do you know so much about Michael himself?" I questioned.

Mr. Valerian grunted deeply. "I inherited a considerable fortune from my father in Greece, as I told you. I came to know Michael when I painted his portrait. He was flattered that I should choose him at once for a subject. I will confess that his grim sense of humor pleased me; witness the lovely bouquet Michael sent to his own funeral —the vast sheaf of spring flowers, mixed with orchids! But Michael had had a strange childhood. He had been born with his mother's fine brain and his father's brute desires! Then fate made his younger sister a weakly girl, upon whom Michael's parents lavished what care and time they had. Michael grew up with a sense of neglect that he felt must one day crush him to earth unless he actively combatted every intent to restrain him—and his desire for living expansively in fine country style was his compensation. It meant everything he had been deprived of as a child. Michael grew into adolescence actually a cunning, sly, savage animal! Then one night Michael's strength took wings. He poisoned his sister, his mother, and his father. He was feeling his power—and his trial proved him master of his fate, to his jungle reasoning. Only a poor immigrant prosecutor stood up to him as a murderer—and Michael's faultless impersonation of a tortured fourteen-year-old boy put this unfortunate public lawyer completely to rout! Michael had won his first contest, and his doom was sealed! He worked a while, went to school, learning, practicing, and then, as inevitably he must, he came to New York to capture the means to retire to the country!"

Mr. Valerian directed the removal from the wall of the huge portrait, which was to go, monument-like, on the bare wall in his own house.

"Just a minute," I demurred. "I have a question, Mr. Valerian. How would you know so much about Michael's younger days—Lady Wintarthur—or did you go as I did to the newspaper library?"

The workmen stood the big portrait up on the floor, and I wondered now that I had ever hated it. There was something so lost and haunted about the thin, talented face. Lisa and I shared a look of dread, not unmixed with pity. Mr. Valerian came to our side and the three of us looked at Michael's face together. Then he answered.

"A most astute question, Mr. Blunt," he said slowly. "I will explain the only way I can. The first man to feel the weight of Michael's cunning was a poor public prosecutor named Henry Denton; an eager immigrant hounded out of his chosen land." Mr. Valerian met our eyes, and his lips twisted wryly. "When I first came to America, long ago; I called myself Henry Denton . . ."

There was silence. As Mr. Valerian dropped a swag of muslin over the portrait of Michael Rawn, the sun suddenly came out and filled the room.

THE END

www.ingramcontent.com/pod-product-compliance
Lightning Source LLC
Chambersburg PA
CBHW020148180626
46810CB00004B/1797